The Mysterious Case
of the Missing Motive

A Redemption Detective Agency Mystery

Books and series by Michele Pariza Wacek

Redemption Detective Agency
(Cozy Mysteries)
A spin-off from the Charlie Kingsley series.
https://MPWNovels.com/r/da_motive

Charlie Kingsley Mysteries
(Cozy Mysteries)
See all of Charlie's adventures here.
https://MPWnovels.com/r/ck_motive

Secrets of Redemption series
(Pychological Thrillers)
The flagship series that started it all.
https://MPWnovels.com/r/rd_motive

Mysteries of Redemption
(Psychological Thrillers)
A spin-off from the Secrets of Redemption series.
https://MPWnovels.com/r/mr_motive

Riverview Mysteries
(standalone Pychological Thrillers)
These stories take place in Riverview, which is near Redemption.
https://MPWnovels.com/r/rm_motive

The Mysterious Case of the Missing Motive

A Redemption Detective Agency Mystery

by Michele Pariza Wacek

For my family, for always believing in me.

Chapter 1

This couldn't possibly be my life.

There was no possible way that I, Emily Hildebrandt, who graduated with honors from high school and then from the University of Wisconsin-Riverview with a 3.8 GPA ... who, as of ten days ago, had a solid job with a good paycheck, a lovely apartment, new car, and fiancé ... was now sitting in a dirty, smelly bus station in Redemption, Wisconsin, trying not to glance at the clock yet again as I continued to wait for my chronically late Aunt Tilde.

On second thought, I realized I should hope she was just late, rather than having mixed up the time I was arriving. Or the day.

Or maybe, she forgot I was coming altogether.

Oh, dear lord. I scrubbed at my face, torn between laughing and crying.

My Aunt Tilde was a character—crazy, lovable, chaotic. In so many ways, she drove me nuts. She was my complete opposite in just about every way.

Yet ... I had always felt a connection with her. She made me feel seen—despite, or maybe because of, her craziness. When I was with her, I felt loved, just as I loved her. But I never felt like I could *live* with her.

Talk about the *Odd Couple*. But worse, because it would be MY life, not a television show.

That said, it was a moot point. No way should I be about to move in with my nutty Aunt Tilde. People like me didn't go through the implosion of their lives and consequent upheaval of everything they've known while being forced to live with their relatives. I was a *responsible* adult. I had done all the responsible, adult, right things. I went to school, studied hard, and picked a useful degree as a business major so I could land a good-paying, solid job … even if it was a little dull. But work is supposed to be dull, right? That's what "being an adult" means—going to work, paying bills, keeping the house neat and tidy. None of these things are fun, but they're all necessary in order to be a responsible adult, like me.

And responsible adults don't need to move in with their Aunt Tilde. Or have their Aunt Tilde give them a job. That isn't how life works.

I must be dreaming. Or trapped in a coma. Otherwise, none of this was making any sense.

If only I hadn't decided to take a closer look at that spreadsheet. Then, I wouldn't have realized something was off. If I had just left it alone, none of this would have happened.

But even as I thought those words, I knew deep down that if I had to do it all over again, I would. Even if it meant losing everything—my job, my home, my car, and my fiancé. Even if it meant I would have no one to turn to except …

"Emily!" Aunt Tilde flung open the door of the station and beamed at me. Her bright-orange hair sparkled in the sunlight and perfectly matched her orange-rimmed glasses, although both clashed horribly with her bright-yellow and red striped shirt. "I'm so sorry I'm late. Traffic was dreadful."

"It's fine. I only just got here," I lied. I seriously doubted small-town Redemption was a snarl of traffic problems, but at that point, I didn't care. I was just relieved she remembered. I got to my feet and started to reach for the suitcase and duffle bag I had tucked under my feet.

But before I could get my hands on them, Aunt Tilde grabbed them. "I can take these if you want to get the rest."

A tight knot seemed to settle in my chest. When I had first moved in with Geoff, my ex, he'd encouraged me to give away most of my belongings. He already had a fully stocked household, so why would we need duplicates of things like plates and towels? Not to mention the apartment was so small, it didn't make sense to clutter it. As usual, he sounded so reasonable, so I ended up selling or donating most of my belongings, including the antique dresser my grandfather had refurbished for me. That, I instantly regretted, along with the set of crystal vases my grandmother gave me as a graduation gift. Now, that regret was doubled. I wondered if Geoff had always viewed me as simply a guest in his space rather than an actual life partner.

I gave my head a quick shake as I reached for the duffle bag. Enough of that. "You don't have to do that. I've got them."

"Nonsense," Aunt Tilde said, trying to juggle both bags. "Go get the rest of your stuff."

A mental image of myself packing what few personal items I had—mostly clothes and bathroom products—flitted across my mind. "This is all I brought. Let me at least take one of them."

I braced myself for questions or condemnations. *What do you mean this is it? I thought you said you were moving here? Who can fit their entire life in one suitcase and one duffle bag?*

But Aunt Tilde just shrugged as she swung the duffle bag toward me. "Smart thinking. Who wants to mess around with a bunch of luggage on a bus anyway?" She started dragging the suitcase to the door, leaving me staring after her in shock.

She paused at the door to glance back at me. "Coming?" I quickly closed my mouth and hurried after her, lugging the duffle bag.

Hot, humid air immediately smacked me in the face as I stepped outside. I shoved a few strands of hair that were sticking to my cheeks back as I increased my pace. For an elderly woman, Aunt Tilde was surprisingly fast, even with my suitcase. "Here we are," she sang out as she approached a light-pink Cadillac that was taking up two spaces, thanks to a very crooked parking job.

I stopped walking, my stomach twisting in on itself. "You have a pink Cadillac?"

She grinned. "I do. Isn't she a beaut?" She patted the trunk lovingly.

Oh no. This was getting worse and worse. "I thought only Mary Kay beauty reps were able to get a pink Cadillac."

"Yep. Isn't it wonderful?" She set my suitcase down and started fiddling with her keys to open the trunk.

This was turning into a nightmare. Was this the job Aunt Tilde had promised me? Helping her with her multi-level marketing business? Was that the reason she was being so cagey about my new job? The idea of sitting in a kitchen surrounded by people I didn't know as I revealed the latest eyeshadow colors was making me break into a cold sweat. "Are you selling Mary Kay?"

She popped the trunk and looked at me like I was crazy. "Heavens no! Do I look like someone who should be giving makeup tips?" She gestured toward her face, which was bare of any color other than a little smeared, pink lipstick, before letting out a rusty laugh. "Good grief." Shaking her head, she turned back to her overflowing trunk.

I didn't move. "If you're not selling Mary Kay, then how did you get one of their cars?"

She waved a hand airily at me. "A friend gave it to me."

A million questions rose up inside me, like how did this "friend" end up with a Mary Kay car? Were they the ones selling Mary Kay? And if they were, why weren't they driving it?

But I forced myself to swallow those questions. Knowing my aunt, I wasn't going to get a straight answer out of her if she wasn't in the mood to give me one. What I needed to do was focus on the positives ... like how my mysterious new job wasn't selling makeup, to start. That was a good thing.

Although if I was being honest, beggars couldn't be choosers. Whatever my aunt had in store for me, I really had no choice but to take it and be grateful for it.

And I *was* grateful. Truly. When I finally called Aunt Tilde three days ago, I was desperate and nearly in tears. Geoff had given me five days to pack my things and move out. "And that's being generous," he told me, his voice sounding so reasonable as he explained how, when couples break up, it's customary for one to leave immediately. Of course, in my case, not only did I not have a job, but I also had no money or legal right to the apartment I had faithfully spent every single Saturday morning cleaning while Geoff lazily enjoyed the newspaper and home-cooked breakfast I made. My name was not on the lease, even though Geoff had assured me it was. Not only that, but the so-called "joint" checking account that I had deposited every one of my checks into wasn't actually joint. It was solely his, and I had merely been a signer on it.

Needless to say, that privilege had also been removed.

The only money to my name was the twenty-seven dollars in my wallet and $333.96 in my personal savings account that I've had for years. Geoff knew nothing about it. He had promised to send me a check once he deducted my half of the last set of bills, but the whole setup had left me feeling uneasy. I reminded myself that despite all his faults, he had always been fair, and there was no reason for him not to be in this situation. It wasn't like he was a thief or anything. He was just thorough, which was something I had always appreciated about him. I was the same way. And I was sure once he found a few minutes to go through all the bills, he would make it right.

No question.

Unfortunately, though, that meant until I got squared away, I only had access to a few hundred dollars, which wasn't going to get me far. Especially if I had to rent a hotel room. It was 1993, after all … even staying in a cheap, rundown hotel wouldn't last long. Both my mother and sister refused to let me stay with them. Well, to be fair, my mother was the one to outright refuse, which I had expected, although it still hurt. My sister told me I was welcome to sleep on her couch for a few days until I got my feet under me. I had a terrible feeling it was going to take longer than a few days to find a job and an apartment I could afford, though. Between that and the exhaustion in my sister's voice as my two nieces screamed at each other in the background, I knew it wasn't an option. I thanked her and told her I would figure something out.

My friend Deena, on the other hand, immediately offered me her couch for as long as I wanted. "It will be fun, like a sleepover," she gushed. As much as I appreciated the offer, Deena had a small, one-bedroom apartment with a boyfriend who stayed over more often than not. Not only that, but he happened to work in the same law firm as Geoff. While Deena might be fine with me staying with her, I suspected her boyfriend wouldn't be nearly as enthusiastic.

And that's how I found myself standing in a parking lot in Redemption, with the noonday summer sun beating down on my head and sweat dripping off my neck, about to get into a pink

Cadillac that I was half-convinced Aunt Tilde had stolen from some nice Mary Kay lady.

When I had called my aunt, there was zero hesitation in her voice as she immediately instructed me to pack up my bags and move to Redemption, where she would not only provide me with a place to live, but a job, as well. I was so grateful and relieved, I nearly burst into tears. Finally, I had somewhere to go that would allow me to lick my wounds and figure out my next steps. I was going to be fine. It was all going to work out.

I should have known there would be a catch.

Aunt Tilde was busy trying to shove my suitcase into her trunk, on top of the mishmash of wrinkled clothes, crumpled fast-food bags, magazines, and cat litter bag, but it wasn't fitting. "Oh, for heaven's sake," she muttered as she tried rearranging things. "Oh, my library books! I need to return them. Emily, can you remind me to do that?"

"Of course," I said, trying not to wince. *Please don't let my job be trying to keep my aunt organized.* Maybe becoming a Mary Kay lady wouldn't be so bad after all.

After a little more pushing and shoving, she finally managed to get my suitcase into the trunk. "Aha! It fits." She turned and gestured toward me. "Here, let's get that other bag in."

I took a few steps forward, still clutching my duffle bag, my eyes fixed again on the bag of cat litter as my stomach filled with a growing sense of horror.

Don't get me wrong ... I liked cats. From a distance, and owned by other people. I didn't have any desire to deal with the mess and hair and everything else that came from owning a pet. Plus, I was fairly certain cats inherently hated me. I had been snarled at and scratched by them more often than not, even from the ones whose owners swore were the friendliest around. "I don't understand what's going on with Princess," my elderly neighbor had fretted a few weeks ago when I stopped by to drop off her mail. "She's the sweetest cat I've ever had," she insisted as Princess hissed and spat at me from the corner.

Again, I reminded myself that beggars couldn't be choosers. If my aunt had a cat, I would just have to figure out a way to not be in the same room with it. With any luck, the cat litter belonged to the Mary Kay lady who was now out of a car. "It doesn't look like there's much room. I can just put it in the backseat."

My aunt clicked her tongue. "Nonsense, there's plenty of room. Besides, Sherlock is in the back."

Sherlock? I craned my neck to peer into the back of the car, but as far as I could tell, it was empty. "Who's Sherlock?"

"Oh, she's one of my partners in my new venture," Aunt Tilde said, taking the duffel bag from me and attempting to shove it into the trunk. "You two will love each other."

I glanced at the backseat again but still didn't see anyone. "New venture?" I asked cautiously.

"You'll see," Aunt Tilde answered mysteriously, giving my bag a final push before slamming the trunk shut with a grunt of relief. "Come on, let's get you home."

I followed her to the front passenger side, still trying to get a peek at the elusive Sherlock. All I saw was what looked like a long, black duffle bag similar to mine. Was Aunt Tilde getting a little senile? I didn't think senility ran in my family, but I was no longer so sure. "Aunt Tilde, I don't see anyone …" I said as I opened up the passenger door.

Just then, the head of a feline popped up from inside the duffle bag, and I let out a shriek.

"Emily, meet Sherlock," Aunt Tilde said with a flourish, getting into the driver's seat.

I didn't move. "Sherlock is a cat?"

"Obviously." She patted the passenger seat next to her.

I still didn't move. "And you're telling me this cat is your partner?"

"I said she's *one* of my partners," Aunt Tilde corrected.

"How can a cat be a partner?"

"You'll see. You just need to have a little faith. Now, let's get you home," she repeated.

I could do nothing but look at her in horror. "What sort of venture is this?"

Aunt Tilde beamed at me. "Trust me. You just have to wait a little bit, and then it will all make perfect sense. Now, get in. We need to get going."

Sherlock blinked at me and yawned, revealing rows and rows of very sharp teeth.

What had I gotten myself into?

Chapter 2

During the entire drive to her house, Aunt Tilde kept up a steady stream of chatter I only half-listened to. It wasn't that I didn't want to pay attention, but I was so tense, my mind kept drifting away. Luckily, Aunt Tilde didn't seem to mind, or even require a response, as she shared the latest gossip and pointed out various locations that I fervently hoped I wouldn't need to remember later.

"Well, here we are," she finally sang out, pulling into the driveway of a nondescript blue ranch house with a detached garage.

I studied it, feeling my chest loosen a bit. It seemed well-maintained, and the yard was in decent shape, although the lawn needed cutting and the bushes trimming. If it was like this on the outside, hopefully, the inside wouldn't be so bad either. I certainly didn't mind pulling my weight and keeping the house and yard neat and tidy, but it would be easier if I wasn't starting with a complete mess.

Aunt Tilde hopped out of the car and circled around to pop the trunk. I followed more slowly after side-eyeing the occupant in the backseat. The cat seemed to be baring her teeth at me.

Not an ideal beginning.

After collecting my bags from the trunk, I started toward the front door. Aunt Tilde, however, was heading toward the garage.

"This way," she called out cheerily, lugging my suitcase.

I froze. The garage? Not even a couch? But then I spotted a staircase on the side leading up to what appeared to be a small apartment.

"It's a little musty," Aunt Tilde said as she fumbled with the key. "I opened the windows this morning, but it probably still needs a good airing out." She pushed open the door before stepping back with a flourish, so I could enter first.

It was small, but it appeared to have all the essentials. The kitchen was complete with a stove, oven, microwave, coffeemaker, fridge, and round kitchen table with three mismatched chairs off to the side. The living room was a large rectangle with a faded floral couch and olive-green recliner. A television sat on an entertainment center that didn't match the coffee table. A large window on the far wall with curtains fluttering in the gentle, humid breeze overlooked the backyard, and a small wooden desk sat in front of it. The bathroom lacked a bathtub, but there was a decent-sized vanity. The bedroom was large enough for a queen bed, dresser, and nightstand.

"It's not much, I know," Aunt Tilde was saying as she shifted her weight from one foot to the other. "But you can use the main house whenever you want, too. The kitchen, bathtub, and washer and dryer, obviously ..."

"It's perfect," I said, and it was. It was more than I ever hoped for. A space of my own. I'd had so many disappointments and failures that I almost couldn't believe something had finally worked out for me.

Her face lit up, and it occurred to me she had been nervous that I might not have been happy with the little apartment. "Here are your keys," she said, handing them to me. I glanced at them, noticing a keychain sporting Snoopy dressed as Sherlock Holmes and Woodstock as his faithful Watson. "One is for the apartment, and the other is for the main house. Dinner will be ready around six, if you want to join me tonight. It's nothing much ... just a casserole and a salad. But, if you'd rather spend a quiet evening here settling in, I've stocked the kitchen with a few basics, too." She went over to the tiny kitchen and began opening cupboards. "Soup, macaroni and cheese, bread, cereal, coffee, tea. Also, there's lunchmeat, cheese, eggs, and milk in the fridge. It's not a lot, but it's something to get you started. If you want, we can go to the grocery store this weekend, and you can stock up. There's plenty of dishes and pots and pans, so you should be set, but if you need anything at all, just give me a holler. Also, the sheets are clean, and there are fresh towels in the bathroom. There's no central air, unfortunately, but there is a window AC unit in the bedroom if it gets too hot to sleep. Oh, and the TV should be hooked up to cable. Let me know if you have any issues. What else … oh, the phone. The number is there, and don't worry about any long-distance charges, unless you're planning on calling Australia or something …"

I put up a hand, suddenly feeling completely overwhelmed by her generosity. No one had done anything like this for me before. "Aunt Tilde, this is too much. I can't pay you anything now, but as soon as I get my feet under me, I'm happy to pay you rent …"

"Nonsense," Aunt Tilde said. "You don't need to pay me any rent."

"But it's too much," I said again. "I need to contribute something …"

"You don't need to do anything," Aunt Tilde said firmly. "It's part of your compensation."

I looked at her in bewilderment. "Compensation for what?"

She gave me an exasperated look. "Your new job, of course."

I gestured around the apartment. "What could I possibly be doing that would include living expenses?"

She flashed me a mysterious smile. "You'll see. It will all become clear on Monday."

"But it's Saturday," I protested. "You're going to make me wait until Monday to know what my new job will be?"

"That gives you plenty of time to rest and settle in," she said. "No sense in rushing anything."

I disagreed, but I suspected I wasn't going to win this battle. "Well, let me at least pay for utilities," I said.

She shook her head. "Absolutely not. It's all part of your compensation package."

I tried not to grit my teeth. I was getting a free apartment that included all utilities along with other perks, such as food in the kitchen and the use of a car, as compensation for a job I knew nothing about. How did I even know if it was a fair deal? "I don't mind helping out," I said. "Maybe I could do some cleaning or organizing for you or something."

Aunt Tilde pursed her lips as she studied me. "Well … it's really not necessary, but if you want, you could help me with the gardening. You know how much of a black thumb I have …"

"Done," I said quickly, feeling myself perk up. I had always loved gardening. Not being able to putter around in a garden was one of the things I'd hated about living in an apartment.

"Well, don't feel like you have to," she said. "There's no need to spend every hour of every day working for me."

"I'm happy to earn my keep," I said. "I can't tell you how grateful I am for what you've done for me. Truly."

She looked at me in surprise. "Emily, we're family! Of course I'm going to be here for you. And it's no trouble at all." She glanced at her watch. "Oh, I didn't realize I've been up here for so long. I better get Sherlock out of the car. She's going to think I abandoned her. And remember, six o'clock, if you'd like to join me for dinner." She grinned at me and started to leave before turning back. "Also, you're helping me far more than I could ever help you." She waved and closed the door before I could respond.

Well. That was certainly nice of her to say, although she couldn't really mean it. Without her help, I could have easily ended up on the streets. I was just going to have to do everything in my power to make it up to her.

Speaking of which, I decided to check out the garden to see how bad of shape it was in. Holding my breath, I moved to the window to peer outside.

It wasn't ... terrible. Overgrown and weedy, but nothing a little elbow grease couldn't fix. I was confident I could whip it into shape.

A movement caught my eye at the line of trees at the back of the property. It was a dog.

It was too far away to see much of it, but it looked big. And mean.

I inhaled sharply. Why was there a dog in Aunt Tilde's yard? Was it a stray? Did it have some disease? Maybe I should warn her. Or maybe we needed to call animal control to come get it.

Before I could figure out the best way to handle it, the dog melted back into the trees. I wasn't sure whether to be relieved or worried. Did that mean it might leap out and attack when we weren't expecting it?

Or ... perhaps it was a neighbor's dog that had gotten loose and was now headed for home.

Regardless, it probably wasn't worth worrying about right that minute, since chances were high I wouldn't see the dog again. If I did, I could deal with it then. Especially since right now, I had other things to focus on, starting with getting myself unpacked and settled in.

I turned away from the window as I rubbed my sweaty hands on my jean shorts. My two bags were sitting in the middle of the living room, next to the coffee table. Even in this tiny apartment, they looked small and insignificant. How could thirty years be reduced into two bags?

Well, it wasn't worth thinking about now. It was time to unpack and organize. I took a step toward my two lonely bags and burst into tears.

Chapter 3

Coffee in hand, I plopped down on the worn couch (which was surprisingly comfortable) and pulled the bright-red phone toward me. I needed to check in with my sister before tackling the garden.

It was nearly ten in the morning, much later than I normally started my weekend. On a "regular" weekend, I would have been up by seven and in the kitchen cooking a big breakfast so it would be ready whenever Geoff got up. But today, I didn't even wake up until after nine. Apparently, I needed the sleep after everything that had happened.

Yesterday, after my crying spell (which seemed to last hours but probably wasn't nearly that long), I had fallen asleep on the floor. When I finally awoke feeling more refreshed and calmer than I had in, well, years, it was after five, and the sun was already starting to cast long shadows across the living-room floor. Initially, I hadn't planned on heading over to Aunt Tilde's for dinner. After all, I still hadn't unpacked. But my stomach was growling, and the thought of a warm, comforting casserole hitting the spot changed my mind.

So, I raced through my unpacking (which really didn't take that long) and was ringing Aunt Tilde's doorbell promptly at six.

"Oh, you don't have to ring the doorbell, just come on in," Aunt Tilde told me as she ushered me inside and pressed a glass of red wine into my hand. If she noticed my puffy face or red-rimmed eyes, she didn't say a word.

After a hot meal, a few glasses of wine, and a grand tour (of a house that was cluttered enough to make my fingers itch to start organizing, but not terrible enough that I couldn't stand being in it), I realized, to my surprise, that I was actually enjoying myself. I had assumed I would want to run out of there as soon as it was polite to leave, but instead, I ended up staying until bedtime. Even Sherlock turned out to not be an issue. The little calico cat sniffed me a few times before settling into a cushioned basket tucked in the corner of the kitchen.

When I finally made it to bed, I had assumed it would take me hours to fall asleep, as I rarely took naps. Instead, I was out the moment my head hit the pillow and slept until late morning.

And now, after a leisurely breakfast and second cup of coffee, I was ready to call Ellen.

"So, you really did it," Ellen said. Again, I could hear my nieces squabbling in the background over which Barbie was whose. "You moved in with Aunt Tilde."

"Well, not exactly with her," I said, dragging the phone toward me so I could sit back on the couch without straining the cord. "More like a little apartment over the garage."

"Seriously? She has an apartment over her garage?"

"I know. It was a surprise to me as well."

"How is it?"

"It's ... cute," I said, looking around at the unmatched furnishings. Perhaps "cute" was a bit of an overstatement.

"Cute, huh?" My sister's voice was dry. She always could see right through me. "Is she lending you a car as well, so you can continue job hunting?"

I cleared my throat. "Actually, she's giving me a job."

"An apartment *and* a job? What's the job?"

"I don't know yet."

"You don't know? How do you not know what your job is?" Now, she sounded perplexed.

"Well ... um ... I guess it's a surprise."

There was a long moment of silence.

"I'll find out Monday," I said, trying to sound more confident than I felt.

The silence stretched out for so long, I would have thought we'd lost the connection, except I could still hear my nieces bickering in the background.

"Emily, you know you didn't have to do this," Ellen finally said. "We could have made it work."

"What? On your couch? How long do you think that would have lasted?"

Her voice was stiff. "I told you, you could stay as long as you needed … until you got your feet under you."

I could feel the tension building between my eyes, and I reached up to massage it. "But what if I need a month? Or longer?"

She scoffed. "Don't be silly. It wouldn't have taken you that long to get another job. You just needed a few days to get your resume together and make some calls."

A dull ache rose in my chest. What Ellen didn't know was that I had already tried that. But somewhere in the middle of leaving my third message for Jane, who used to be one of my coworkers but now worked at a different firm, a funny feeling in my stomach began to take root. I was being ignored. While some never called me back, the ones I managed to get on the phone made excuses and hung up as quickly as they could. Finally, I was able to pin down Beth, who I had served on the same volunteer committees with, and she basically confirmed what that funny feeling was telling me—I was being blackballed.

But I couldn't tell my sister that. Ellen didn't even know the truth about why I was let go. I had been way too embarrassed to tell her. How could I? Her life was perfect, and mine was a train wreck. I didn't think I could bear it if she realized how stupid and gullible I had been. Or worse, if she felt sorry for me.

"And what if it wasn't that easy? What if it took months? Then what?"

There was a long pause. "Emily, I …" she started to say. But then, she stopped herself and sucked in a deep breath. "We would have figured something out." There was an edge to her voice I hadn't heard before.

I rolled my eyes. "I appreciate that. Truly. But I think this is easier for everyone."

"It's not easier for you," she argued. "How are you going to job search from Redemption?"

I wound my finger around the telephone cord. "I can mail resumes and make phone calls from Redemption."

"What about interviews?"

"I'll figure something out. Aunt Tilde will probably let me borrow her car."

She let out a loud sigh. "But what about when you get the job? It's going to be a pain for you to move back. And how are you going to be able to job hunt if you're working full-time?"

I rolled my eyes. "Ellen, I'm forty-five minutes away. It's not like I moved to Florida. It might take me a little longer to find a new job living here, but I'm sure it will be fine."

There was another long pause. "Emily, what did you get yourself into?"

"It's fine. It's going to be fine." Maybe if I kept telling myself that, it really would be.

"How is it going to be fine? This is Aunt Tilde we're talking about. Who knows what sort of job she's gotten you! It might not even be legal."

I felt a jolt in my stomach. "I'm sure it's legal." Visions of the pink Cadillac filled my mind. I quickly pushed them away.

"How can you be so sure? What about that underground gambling network she created?"

"It wasn't exactly gambling," I said. "More like … friendly poker games."

"She had a member of the Russian mafia as a regular."

"We don't know that he was really part of the Russian mafia," I argued. "He could have been exaggerating."

"Like he exaggerated about putting a hit on one of her teacher friends because she cleaned him out that one night?"

Oh. I had forgotten about that. "Well, she's still alive." *I think.*

"Even if this does end up being on the up and up," Ellen continued, "it's still a backwards step for you." She seemed to be completely ignoring the screaming that had risen in volume in the background. "You're stuck in Redemption, and we all know how strange that little town is. It's going to be hard for you to find a decent job, especially if you're going to be running around doing God knows what for Aunt Tilde. And that means your career is going to suffer. Don't even get me started on your love life."

"My love life is the least of my concerns," I said quickly, deliberately ignoring everything she said about my career. What she didn't know was that my career was already ruined, so it didn't matter where I lived. "I have no plans to jump into another relationship."

"Geoff is a jerk. But that doesn't mean you should never date again."

Says the woman with the perfect husband, I thought, trying not to gnash my teeth together. I knew Ellen meant well, but that didn't keep the jealously from flaring up inside me. "Well, I at least need a break. And that's all this is … a break. I haven't had a vacation, a real vacation, in years. So, maybe I should look at this as an opportunity. I can take a little break and get my head on straight before taking the time to find the right job. Then, once I do, I'll move back. Okay?"

"Just don't take too long of a break," she said before softening her voice. "I agree you've been working way too hard. You deserve a little time off. But if you let it drag on too long, you know as well as I do it's going to be a lot tougher getting back on that career ladder again."

I rolled my eyes again. Ellen was a stay-at-home mom with a husband who adored her and had a great job. What did she know about climbing a career ladder? "I promise I won't take too long of a break, mom."

"Remember, you're always welcome here," Ellen said.

Even though I knew it would be a ridiculously bad idea, it still warmed my heart to hear her offer. "I appreciate that."

***

I gave a particularly stubborn weed a vicious yank before pausing to wipe the sweat off my brow.

I had been out in the garden for several hours, trying to work out the years-old resentment that had crept into my chest while speaking to Ellen. After all, it wasn't Ellen's fault my life was a mess while hers was perfect. Well, maybe not perfect perfect, as there was a lot of screaming going on in her house. But what would anyone expect with two girls under six? At least she didn't have to work. She was able to raise her two little daughters in a beautiful home with a nice backyard while being fully supported by a wonderful husband.

I was happy for her. Truly. I just didn't understand how she could do everything wrong and still have everything work out for her, while I did everything right and was currently living in an apartment over my aunt's garage.

Ellen and I were always exact opposites. She was the rebel—the one who skipped school regularly, would steal our mother's liquor and cigarettes, and party all night. I was the one who stayed home and cleaned up the vomit after our mother passed out (again) in the living room, did my homework, and got straight As.

I landed a scholarship to the University of Wisconsin-Riverview. She graduated high school by the skin of her teeth. I obsessed over following the rules. The only time she cared about the rules was when she decided to break them.

Eventually, she cleaned herself up. She enrolled in Riverview Community College and became a medical technician, which is where she wound up meeting her future husband, who just happened to be a heart surgeon.

As happy as I was for her, I couldn't help but feel a tiny bit resentful at how quickly and easily everything fell into place for her.

I jerked at another difficult weed. Maybe it all worked out for Ellen because she was drop-dead gorgeous, with her strawberry-blonde hair, dark-blue eyes, heart-shaped face, and pouty lips. Not to mention her perfect Barbie-doll body, which she had managed to maintain even after giving birth to two adorable children. Could I really blame Ian for taking one look at her and falling head over heels?

I, on the other hand, was far from gorgeous. I would probably call myself "average." Secretly, I considered myself a copy (well, more like a copy of a copy of a copy) of my sister—like so many copies made the original that they became blurred and out of focus. My hair was brown with blond highlights, my eyes blue-gray, and my face narrow with high cheekbones (the latter probably being my best feature). My figure was definitely not similar to Ellen's, though, as I was more straight and narrow, rather than curvy.

But all that aside, I truly thought if I did everything right, life would reward me.

Yeah, right.

I wrestled one particularly large weed out of the ground, nearly falling on my butt when I finally succeeded. Sweat trickled down my back, causing my shirt to stick to my skin. My back hurt and my legs were cramping up.

And I was loving every minute of it.

A honeybee buzzed nearby, and a couple of birds chirped happily. The air was rich with the scents of damp earth and green plants. It had been so long since I'd had my fingers in the soil, I hadn't realized how much I missed it.

Despite Aunt Tilde's comments about having a black thumb, her garden was anything but barren. Rather, it was a jungle gone wild, wherein weeds fought with flowers to get the upper hand.

I suspected it would take at least a few sessions to get it under control enough for me to even see what was growing, much less start cultivating the plants that seemed determined to outwit the weeds. It didn't help that I kept finding things buried and neglected in the grass—a broken sprinkler, a faded blue bucket, a chipped croquet mallet, a tennis racket with a bent handle, a silver bowl, and a deflated volleyball. There was even a wheelbarrow missing a front wheel and a rusted bicycle. I finally started collecting all the various items and putting them in a corner near the house, figuring I would deal with putting them (or better yet, throwing them away) later.

I stood up, taking a moment to stretch my back and pull my tee shirt away from my sweaty body. It was *really* hot. I headed over to the glass outdoor table where a tall glass of lemonade sat. Aunt Tilde had thoughtfully brought it out for me.

I had just reached for the glass when something caught my eye. It was the dog.

I froze, hand on the glass. It was standing in the shade of the trees in the back of the yard, watching me. His mouth was open, and his tongue lolled out. Probably because he was getting ready to eat me.

This was my worst nightmare.

What should I do? Could I run? I was closer to the house than he was, so maybe I could get away. But didn't I once read that you shouldn't run away from dogs? Or was that bears? Now, I couldn't remember, but my legs felt so weak and rubbery, I wasn't even sure if I *could* run.

Maybe I should scream. If I was loud enough, maybe Aunt Tilde would hear me and call for help. I imagined her running out of the house brandishing a shotgun, firing one off as she charged the dog.

Or, maybe more likely, she would come running out with a piece of steak to try to coax it away and get her arm bit off instead.

No, that wouldn't work either. I was going to have to figure this out myself.

The dog hadn't moved an inch. It stood in the shade, watching me. As I stared back, I saw his tail swish gently.

Was that a tail wag? That was good, right? Or maybe all dogs swished their tail when they were getting ready to attack. Although … to be honest, he didn't really look dangerous. His yellow fur was matted and filthy, and he seemed too thin. His mouth opened further as he continued to pant.

Wait a minute. Maybe he wasn't thinking about eating me after all. Maybe he was simply thirsty.

I looked around the backyard and saw the silver bowl sitting in the heap with the rest of the forgotten items.

Slowly, I started inching toward the bowl. The dog didn't move, just continued to watch me. Once I got the bowl, I had to creep my way over to the hose to fill it with water. All the while, the dog simply stared at me, his tail swishing from side to side.

Of course, once the bowl was full, I was going to have to figure out some way to get it closer to him—without triggering him to go for my throat, that was. Carefully, I moved toward him, my entire body tense, praying he wouldn't attack.

The dog stayed where he was, although his eyes moved from me to the bowl. When water sloshed out of it, he licked his lips.

Finally, when I was as close as I dared, I put the bowl on the grass and scampered away, crossing my fingers that I didn't just make the worst mistake of my life.

It took him a minute, but he eventually trotted forward, eyes on the bowl the whole time. He lowered his head and began to noisily drink, water flying everywhere.

I squinted, trying to see if there was a collar on him, but as far as I could tell, there was nothing. Although considering how bad his coat looked, I was starting to doubt he belonged to a neighbor. If he did, that person should probably be arrested for animal neglect. That poor animal deserved a lot better.

Once the dog drained the bowl, he lifted his head, gave me a quick tail wag, then turned and trotted off, melting back into the trees.

I stayed where I was, making sure it wasn't a trap, and he wasn't going to come barreling out of the trees and lunge for my neck. But there was nothing besides the chirping of birds. I wondered if I should call someone, maybe animal control. It couldn't be good to have a stray dog loose around the neighborhood. Of course, it was Sunday, so I suspected no one would be there. Tomorrow, then.

I finally moved toward the table to take a drink of my lemonade, making a mental note to fill the bowl one more time before I went in for the night.

Chapter 4

"Tada!" Aunt Tilde said as she opened the door of an unmarked business at the end of a strip mall. "Welcome to the Redemption Detective Agency."

I blinked as I looked around. "The Redemption Detective Agency?"

She grinned at me as she nodded.

"This is your business?" I asked.

"Whose else would it be?"

"But …" There was so much wrong, I couldn't figure out where to start. "There's no sign on the door," I finally said, although that seemed like the least of the issues.

"Don't worry about that," she said. "Just a little hiccup."

"Not having a sign is a hiccup? How will clients find you?"

"That's not important right now," Aunt Tilde said, pulling me inside. "What do you think?" She made a flourish with her arm.

I gave my head a quick shake, wondering if that would change the picture in front of me.

It didn't.

We were in a large room at the end of a strip mall that also housed a dry-cleaning business, a used bookstore, and a pawn store advertising that they "buy gold!" The walls were a dingy white, and the floors were covered in dark carpeting, although it was difficult to tell what the color actually was. Brown? Black? Dark blue? A mix of the three? Impossible to tell. Against the far wall was a low built-in counter, which had a coffee maker and a large water jug on it. There was a swinging door in the center next to what looked like a large, plywood-covered hole in the wall, and on the far right was a long hallway. A cat tree stood in front of the hole, and Sherlock immediately made herself comfortable in it the moment Aunt Tilde released her from her crate.

There were four desks, one in each corner, with a couple of bookshelves and metal filing cabinets against the side walls. The bookshelves contained not only books, but other odd objects, such as a collection of mugs and a half-dead plant. There was a faint, rather unpleasant odor, as well, that I couldn't immediately identify.

"As you can see, there's lots of space," Aunt Tilde said. "The downside is no separate offices. At least not yet. But we can make it work."

I was still trying to get my head around the fact that Aunt Tilde owned a detective agency ... and what precisely that meant for this mysterious job I was supposed to be getting. "What's over there?" I pointed to the hallway to the right.

"Bathrooms," Aunt Tilde said.

I pointed to the swinging door. "What about there?"

"Just the break room."

Break room? With a swinging door? "Then why is there a coffee pot and water jug out here?"

"Well, we can't have the clients wandering around in our break room, can we?" She let out a guffaw. "Besides, it's more convenient to have them out here."

"What about the detectives? Where are they?" I asked.

Aunt Tilde gave me an exasperated look. "Silly. We're the detectives."

I stared at her. "*We're* the detectives?"

"Of course." She spun around again. "So, tell me ... what do you think of your new job?"

"My new job?" Oh no. My worst suspicions were coming true. "I'm not a detective. I don't know the first thing about being a detective."

She waved a hand. "What are you talking about? You're a natural. You figured out who was embezzling money at your last job."

"Which is what got me fired."

"Well, you don't have to worry about that here. Here, we encourage you to solve all the crimes you want."

I couldn't believe this was happening. I felt like I had just stepped into an episode of *The Twilight Zone*. "You're a retired nurse. When did you become a detective?"

"Oh, you know me. I've always loved reading detective books. Give me a good Sherlock Holmes or Agatha Christie mystery, and I'm in heaven."

I gave her a sharp look. "Reading mysteries is not the same as solving them."

"But I usually can," she insisted. "You know I have a knack for it."

"That's still not the same," I said. "In this case, you're being paid to solve crimes for people. Like a private investigator." Another thought occurred to me, and I frowned. "Don't you need a license to be a PI?"

She spread her arms out. "This is the Redemption Detective Agency, not the Redemption Private Investigator Agency."

"So, that's a no. This 'business' doesn't have all the necessary and legal licenses, does it?"

She beamed at me. "I told you you're a natural."

I started to rub my temples. Ellen was going to have a field day when I told her my new job was working for Aunt Tilde's unlicensed private detective agency.

Then another thought struck me. "Is that why there's no sign? Because this isn't legal?"

Aunt Tilde patted my arm. "See, this is why we make such a good team."

I tried not to focus on how she wasn't answering any of my questions. "What are you talking about?"

"Well, along with being a detective, I was also hoping you would be our office manager."

I wasn't sure if I heard her correctly. "You want me to be the office manager?"

"Well, as you know, I'm not very good at all those pesky details. I was hoping you would come in and really whip everything into shape."

"Everything?" I looked around at the four empty desks and Sherlock, who was still sitting on top of the cat tree, like she was surveying her domain. What did I get myself into? "How big is the Redemption Detective Agency?"

"Well, we're still in the start-up phase. But we're growing!"

I gave her a skeptical look. "Start-up? What's your annual revenue?"

She rolled her eyes. "I just said we're a start-up. We haven't been around for a year yet."

"Okay, so what's your revenue for the month?"

Aunt Tilde didn't answer. Instead, she began busying herself by the coffeepot.

"What about the week?"

She pulled the empty pot out. "I should go rinse this out, so I can get some coffee started …"

I planted myself in front of her, arm crossed. "IS there any revenue?"

"Define 'revenue.'"

"Money coming in the door. Typically paid by clients." She didn't look at me while she fussed with the coffee filters. "You do have clients, right?"

She jerked her head up. "Of course we have clients. Don't be absurd."

I refused to be deterred. "Do they …"

The tinkling of the bell on the door interrupted me. "Hello, hello!" a chipper voice from behind me said.

Aunt Tilde's face instantly relaxed. "Mildred! Come in and meet Emily."

I turned and nearly passed out from the cloud of floral perfume wafting toward me from the newcomer. From what I could tell, based on my watering eyes, Mildred was the exact opposite of Aunt Tilde. Whereas Aunt Tilde wore an oversized bright-yellow shirt with a Pepsi logo across the front that clashed with her orange hair and glasses, Mildred was dressed in a pressed green pantsuit. Her gray, permed hair looked freshly styled, like she had recently visited the hairdresser.

"Emily! It's so lovely to see you again." Mildred reached out to give my hands a squeeze. There was something about her that was familiar, but I couldn't put my finger on it. "I don't know if you remember me. We met … oh, it's been a few years now, hasn't it, Tilde? I was still teaching, wasn't I?"

Aunt Tilde tapped her lips. "Yeah, I think so. It must be at least fifteen years ago now."

"Oh my, has it been that long?" Mildred said.

"Wait a minute," I said, staring at Mildred. "I remember you. You were part of that underground gambling ring, weren't you?"

Mildred stared at me. "Underground gambling ring? Heavens. It was just a little friendly poker, that's all."

"There's nothing illegal about a little friendly poker game," Aunt Tilde echoed.

Again, I refused to be deterred. "But weren't you threatened by a guy in the Russian Mafia?"

"Dmitry? Oh my, I forgot about him," Mildred said. "Now that you say it, he did mention something about getting even with me. He was always such a sore loser."

"Dmitry was all talk," Aunt Tilde scoffed. "Russian mafia ... ha! He wishes he was in the Russian mafia."

I wasn't sure if I was relieved or worried about the explanation.

"Anyway," Mildred continued. "I'm so glad you're here. I've got someone I want you to meet." There was a gleam in her eye that made me instantly shudder.

"Oh, I appreciate the offer, but I'm taking a break from men," I said.

Mildred squeezed my hand harder. "Nonsense. You need to get right back on the horse. That's the best way to get over a bad breakup."

Bad breakup? I swiveled my head toward Aunt Tilde, but she was very focused on opening the can of coffee.

"Jerome is perfect for you," Mildred said, patting my arm. Her hands were dry and powdery. "He teaches chemistry at the high school. Very smart and handsome, and he's single. I know he would love to meet you."

"Wow, he sounds great," I said faintly, feeling my heart sink into my shoes. I could just imagine what single chemistry teacher Jerome would be like if he needed someone like Mildred to find dates for him. "But honestly, I'm really not looking to date right now."

She patted my arm again. "I'll make the introduction, and then you can decide. I'm sure once you meet him, you'll change your mind."

"You really don't need to trouble yourself," I said.

"Oh, no trouble at all," she said. "Whatever I can do to help. You've had such a terrible run of bad luck. I still can't believe what those horrible Duckworths did to you." She shuddered. "But don't worry. We'll take good care of you."

"Wait, you know about the Duckworths?" A lot of people didn't realize I worked directly for the Duckworths, one of the richest and most powerful families in Wisconsin. They were based out of Riverview and connected to many local businesses, either directly or indirectly. I was the office manager for Duckworth Brokerage and Investments, which had satellite offices throughout the state, but my job was at the main office. "How did you …" I whirled around to face Aunt Tilde, who at least had the grace to look slightly ashamed of herself. "Who else did you tell?"

"No one really," Aunt Tilde mumbled.

"Ahem," Mildred said.

"Oh, you're like family," Aunt Tilde said, waving her hand.

I gave her a hard look. "Anyone else 'like family'?"

"Nora," Mildred said, her voice still chipper.

"Who wants coffee?" Aunt Tilde asked, holding up the empty coffeepot.

"Who is Nora?" I asked Aunt Tilde.

"She owns Read It Again," Mildred answered.

I was still staring at Aunt Tilde. "You told the person who owns the used bookstore? What about the owners of the dry cleaner, or the pawnshop?"

"Don't be silly," Aunt Tilde said. "Nora is like family, too. She brings us books to read."

"Oh, so that's what you're doing with the time you're not spending with the clients you don't have? Reading books?" I asked.

"I told you, we're a startup," Aunt Tilde said with a huff. "It takes a while to get a new business off the ground."

I tried not to roll my eyes. "Any other family members I should know about?"

"The church group," Mildred said. "They're our spiritual family, after all. Oh, and they're praying for you."

I covered my eyes. Apparently, everyone in Redemption now knew about my humiliation.

I felt a warm hand on my arm. "Emily, I'm truly sorry. I didn't know you wanted me to keep it to myself," Aunt Tilde said.

I kept my palms over my eyes. "I told you not to tell anyone."

"Actually, you told me not to tell Ellen or your mother, and I didn't say anything to either of them," Aunt Tilde said.

"Why don't you want everyone to know?" Mildred asked. "What they did to you was dreadful. You should be screaming it from the rooftops."

"It's … complicated." How could I explain my embarrassment when I realized my loyalty was being repaid by betrayal? I had naively thought because I had the Duckworths' back, they would have mine.

Instead, they had thrown me under the bus.

"How is it complicated? They should be ashamed of themselves," Mildred said. "I think they should …"

"And they will be," Aunt Tilde said firmly, her eyes searching my face intently. "There's plenty of time for that. Right now, you have enough on your plate with the move and your new job." She shot Mildred a meaningful look. Mildred seemed to have gotten the message and closed her mouth.

"I think it's time for some coffee, don't you?" Aunt Tilde's voice was bright as she waved the empty coffeepot and headed for the hallway that led toward the bathrooms.

"Why are you going that way?" I asked. "Why not use the break room?"

Mildred stared at me. "Break room? What are you talking about? We have a break room? Since when?" she asked Aunt Tilde.

Aunt Tilde looked a little flustered. "Oh, she's talking about … there." She pointed toward the swinging door.

Mildred looked more confused. "You mean that greasy kitchen filled with cockroaches?"

I was still stuck on Mildred's words—specifically, the "we" in the "We have a break room?" question, but the mention of cockroaches drove that out of my head. "Cockroaches? Are you serious?"

"Just don't go in the kitchen, and you should be fine," Mildred advised.

"You rented a place crawling with cockroaches?" I asked Aunt Tilde.

"It's really not a big deal," Aunt Tilde said quickly. "We just have to make some modifications."

"Is this the real reason the coffee and water are out here?" I asked, but Aunt Tilde had disappeared down the hallway.

Mildred nodded her head. "And why we keep the coffee mugs over there," she said, pointing at one of the shelves in the bookcase filled with upside down mugs.

I thought about the sandwich I had brought for lunch, which was still in my purse, and considered going out to eat instead.

"Why is the kitchen full of cockroaches? What happened in there?" I asked as Aunt Tilde appeared with the coffee pot full of water and headed over to the drip machine.

"It's probably because it's cursed," Mildred said casually as she moved to the shelf to select a mug.

"*Cursed?*" Ellen was going to have a field day with this bit of information.

"Not cursed like Redemption," Aunt Tilde called out as she finished filling the machine with water.

This was getting better and better. "How many types of curses are there?"

Redemption, Wisconsin, had a long-standing reputation of strange and unexplained events occurring on a regular basis. Some people have called the town cursed, although I wasn't necessarily one of them. I wasn't sure I believed in curses or ghosts or hauntings, although Redemption had plenty of stories about all of that.

It all started back in 1888, when all the adults disappeared seemingly overnight, leaving only the children behind. No one was ever able to find any explanation for what had happened to the adults. The children claimed they didn't know. They just woke up one morning, and all the adults were gone. The mystery remained unsolved to this day, along with many other unsolved murders and disappearances … far more than a town the size of Redemption ought to have.

Aunt Tilde flipped the switch on the coffeemaker and dried her hands on her blue and white striped pants. "You know how there's always that one restaurant that's constantly changing hands, and no one can figure out how to make it work, despite it being in a seemingly great location? Cursed like that."

I stared at her, feeling a growing sense of horror rise in my gut. "You rented this place knowing that other businesses failed here?" Maybe I needed to brush up my resume sooner rather than later, as it seemed even less likely Aunt Tilde's experiment was going to work.

"Restaurants," Aunt Tilde said, moving to the shelf to select a mug. "Not detective agencies."

"And the reason why they failed may have been the cockroaches, not the location," Mildred volunteered as she waited for the coffee to finish brewing.

"Or they were just lousy at running a restaurant," Aunt Tilde said. "Like the last one. Why anyone would try and compete against Aunt May's Diner in this town is beyond me. That place is an icon."

"Remember the Mexican restaurant that was owned by a couple of non-Mexicans?" Mildred asked. "They tried to market themselves as 'authentic.' Honestly, what was authentic about them?"

"Good thing there's a Chi-Chi's not too far away," Aunt Tilde said, and Mildred agreed. I wasn't sure if Chi-Chi's would be considered authentic Mexican food either, but I was fairly certain their kitchens would be much cleaner.

Sherlock yawned, showing all her sharp little teeth as she looked around the office, tail flickering. I wondered if she was keeping an eye out for any stray cockroaches.

Maybe it wouldn't be so bad to have a cat around after all.

"Coffee is ready, if you want to grab a cup," Aunt Tilde said, gesturing toward the mugs.

I eyed the mugs, but didn't move toward them. "Maybe later."

"It's completely fine," Aunt Tilde said, reading my mind. "It's really not a big deal, once you make a few adjustments."

"We've never seen a cockroach on that shelf," Mildred piped in, which somehow didn't reassure me.

I opened my mouth to answer when the phone rang.

Chapter 5

"The phone is ringing," Mildred said excitedly. "Maybe it's a new client."

"Maybe," Aunt Tilde said. "See, Emily? You're already bringing us luck."

I didn't point out it just as easily could be a telemarketer or bill collector looking for payment. Why spoil their excitement, when they would know as soon as one of them picked up the phone?

"Are you going to get it, Emily?" Aunt Tilde asked.

I stared at her in astonishment. "Me? Why do you want me answering the phone?"

"You are the office manager, right?" Aunt Tilde said. "Isn't that what office managers do?"

The phone rang again. Actually, more accurately, four phones were ringing. There was a phone on each of the four desks, and they were all ringing in unison.

"Well, sure," I said. "But it's my first day. I haven't been trained. I don't know what to say."

"What are you talking about? You've been trained," Aunt Tilde said, waving her hand. "You've been working as an office manager, right? You know the drill."

"No, I don't mean trained as an office manager, I mean …" I was interrupted by the phones ringing again.

"Emily, you have to answer it," Mildred said, her voice in a panic. "You don't want our new client to go away."

"Yes, answer it," Aunt Tilde said.

I shot Aunt Tilde an exasperated look. Clearly, I had a number of things I was going to have to discuss with her, including defining Mildred's role in the Redemption Detective Agency and determining who was in charge of answering phones. I moved to the closest desk to pick up the receiver.

"No, that's not your desk," Mildred said, gesturing to the one closest to the coffeemaker. "Tilde, didn't we decide that was going to be Emily's desk?"

"No, I we thought it would be better if she was closer to the door, so she could greet the clients when they come in," Aunt Tilde said.

Mildred shook her head, causing her gray curls to flip around her head. "No, I'm pretty sure we decided she should be closer to the coffeemaker."

"Guys, does it really matter?" I asked, noting I was also going to have to add to my list of discussion topics that being an office manager wasn't a glorified office assistant.

The phone rang again. "Emily, what are you waiting for?" Mildred cried out. "Answer the phone."

I snatched up the closest phone. "The Redemption Detective Agency, Emily speaking."

Aunt Tilde poked Mildred with her elbow. "See? I told you she would be a natural." I tried not to roll my eyes.

"So this is for real?" It was a woman's voice, and she sounded both skeptical and abrupt.

"I'm sorry?"

"Why are you sorry?" Mildred asked. I turned away from her.

"This is the Redemption Detective Agency?" Now, the voice sounded impatient.

"Yes. Can I help you?"

"Are you actually detectives?"

I had no idea how to answer that. "Are you looking for a detective?"

There was a snort. "I wouldn't be calling if I wasn't."

"See, it is a client," Mildred said.

"What kind of case?" Aunt Tilde asked.

I waved at them both to be quiet. "What kind of help are you looking for, exactly?"

There was a pause on the other end. "I'm … I don't know what to do … I'm at the end of my rope …"

"What's the case?" Mildred said in a stage whisper so close to me, I jumped.

"What was that?" the voice on the other end snapped.

"Nothing," I said, trying to shove both Mildred and Aunt Tilde away. "Just the cat."

"The cat? What kind of nonsense is this? I should have known not to call."

"Wait, don't hang up …" But it was too late.

"What happened?" Mildred asked. "Why did they hang up?"

I willed myself to take a breath. "Because she heard you whispering."

"How could she hear me?" Mildred asked. "I was whispering. And why would that make her hang up?"

"You should have invited her to come in, so we could have talked to her," Aunt Tilde said.

"And that's why I shouldn't have been the one to take the call," I said. "I don't know anything about The Redemption Detective Agency, other than our office is in the same place as a bunch of failed restaurants, and we apparently have giant cockroaches as roommates."

"She's got a point," Mildred said to Aunt Tilde.

"You're right," Aunt Tilde said, pulling out one of the chairs and settling herself down. "What do you want to know?"

I took a moment to push the hair out of my face and take another breath. I wasn't used to being told I was right, and it made me feel a little unsteady, like I was trying to get my sea legs. "Well, first of all, why do we have four desks? Who else works here?"

"Oh, that's easy," Aunt Tilde said cheerfully. "You, me, Mildred," Mildred wiggled her fingers at me. "And Nora."

"From the bookstore?" I asked.

"The one and same," Aunt Tilde said.

"Why does Nora need a desk? Doesn't she have her own desk in her bookstore?" *Please don't say you gave her a desk because she brings books over …*

"She has to have somewhere to sit when she brings us books," Mildred said.

I briefly closed my eyes.

"We were thinking her desk should be over there," Aunt Tilde said, pointing to the one next to the front door. "Mine would be there," she pointed to the desk on the other side of the hallway.

"I thought we agreed that would be my desk," Mildred said.

"No, that's always been my desk," Aunt Tilde said.

"But I need to be closer to the bathroom," Mildred said.

I held my hand up. "We'll figure out the desk situation later. Quite honestly, this isn't a great setup anyway. We need a conference room or a table … a place to meet with clients …"

Aunt Tilde's eyes went wide, and she gently slapped Mildred on her arm. "A conference room! Emily, you're a genius!"

"Don't call me a genius yet. I haven't quite figured out how to put one in," I said. "The kitchen would make the most sense, but obviously, that's not going to happen anytime soon. But anyway, who are the detectives? You two?"

"And you," Aunt Tilde said, beaming at me. "I told you, we're all detectives. The Redemption Detective Agency doesn't discriminate."

"Okay, but …"

The tinkling of the bell on the door interrupted me. A woman with her arms full was fumbling at the door. "Oh, for heaven's sake," I heard her mutter while almost dropping a closed Tupperware container as she juggled it and a very large purse.

"Pat! You came by," Aunt Tilde said, hurrying to the door to take the Tupperware container. A white head popped out of the purse and let out a yip. "And hello, Tiki! Don't think I forgot about you." Tiki stretched her neck out as far as it would go and gave Aunt Tilde a little lick.

"Of course I came by," Pat sniffed. She nodded to Mildred before plucking a wiggling Tiki out of her purse. "You told me your niece was going to be here, and I wanted to welcome her." She set Tiki down, who greeted Aunt Tilde and Mildred before racing over to Sherlock, who jumped down off her cat tower to nose the little white teacup poodle. Tiki was dressed in a pink Hello Kitty shirt and had pink ribbons on her ears. "And I brought cookies."

Aunt Tilde's face perked up as Pat took the Tupperware container from her.

My first impression of Pat was that she was round. She was plump, with a round face, round, black-rimmed glasses, and short, no-nonsense brown hair that was turning gray. "You must be Emily," she said as she came toward me, opening up the container. "Charlie's famous chocolate chip cookies."

"Who's Charlie?" I asked, helping myself to one.

"Charlie Kingsley," Mildred said. "Only the most famous detective in Redemption. She's a legend. She helped get to the bottom of the mystery around the vampire living next door to me."

I stared at her. "You had a *vampire* living next door to you?"

"It all worked out in the end, so you don't have to worry about being attacked by a vampire," Mildred said.

"I helped Charlie solve a couple of her cases, too," Aunt Tilde said. Pat rolled her eyes. "In fact, she was the inspiration for opening up the Redemption Detective Agency."

"And Charlie was sorry she couldn't come by for your … grand opening, which is why she sent cookies. Oh, and this." Pat put the container down and started rummaging through her large purse before finally locating two small, white, paper bags with a purple "Charlie's Concoctions" stamp on it. "Tea," she explained as she handed them to me.

I looked at her questioningly. "Tea?"

"Charlie has a tea business. She grows herbs and flowers in her backyard and makes custom blends with them," Pat said. "Those are two of her most popular blends, Lemon Lavender and Deep Sleep. They're both very relaxing."

"Um … thank you," I said, wondering why someone I had never met would give me tea.

"Her teas are fabulous," Mildred said. "I'm a regular customer. And she can even make special blends if you're having health issues."

"Anytime you're feeling stressed, just brew up a cup of that tea," Pat said. "You'll be amazed at how much better you'll feel."

It suddenly dawned on me that these weren't just "Welcome to Redemption" housewarming gifts. "Did my aunt happen to mention anything that would make you think I needed something to help with stress?"

Pat looked a little uncomfortable as she eyed Aunt Tilde. "Well … after everything you've gone through over the past couple of weeks, it would be perfectly natural to have trouble sleeping and stress."

Great. Another stranger who knew my life story. Was there anyone in this town who didn't?

"And it's not like it's a big secret that you're … wound up a little tight," Aunt Tilde said, coming closer. "Especially now, I figured you could use some relaxation."

My mouth dropped open. "What do you mean, everyone knows I'm wound up a little tight? I just met everyone today!"

"I didn't tell everyone that," Aunt Tilde said. "Just Charlie, because I thought her tea would help."

"No, she mostly just focused on what those horrible Duckworths did to you," Mildred said. "And what your fiancé did. Good riddance to all of them."

I wasn't sure if that was better or worse.

Pat cleared her throat as she picked up the container of cookies and carried them to the coffeemaker. "Anyway. Let me know if the tea helps. There's plenty more if you need a refill. Are there any mugs?"

"Oh, over here," Aunt Tilde said, pointing to the shelf as she followed Pat to the coffeemaker and snatched up the cookies.

Pat gave her a funny look. "Why are the mugs on a shelf far away from the coffee? And what are you doing with the cookies?"

"Just moving them to a better location," Aunt Tilde said airily as she carried them to the desk that was furthest away from the coffeemaker.

"Trust me, they're safer over there," Mildred said, handing her a mug.

Pat eyed her. "Safer from what?"

"It's nothing to be worried about," Aunt Tilde sang out.

Pat looked at the mug, then at the coffee. "Can I drink the coffee?"

"Of course," Mildred held up her own mug. "Tilde made it fresh this morning." She took a drink and wiggled her eyebrows over her mug.

Pat looked deeply skeptical but poured herself a cup, then doctored it with the powdered cream and sugar.

"Any cases yet?" Pat asked as she stirred her coffee.

"We almost had one today, but she hung up on Emily," Mildred said.

Pat gave her a strange look. "Why is Emily answering the phone? Isn't it her first day?"

"Exactly my point," I said, pointing at Aunt Tilde, who was scarfing down a cookie.

Aunt Tilde shrugged. "She has to learn somehow. Might as well let her get started sooner than later."

"A little training first would be helpful," I said. Even though I knew it wasn't my fault, I was still feeling bad about what happened with the caller. I could still hear the desperation in her voice. She clearly needed help, but what could I do now?

"So, as the new office manager, you can help set up our training program," Aunt Tilde said.

Pat and I exchanged a look. "I don't envy you," she said.

"I don't envy me either," I said.

The bell above the door tinkled again. "Good morning! Oh, my goodness, it's like a party in here."

A petite woman who looked like she was about a decade older than me entered the office carrying several books. She had long, dark-red, frizzy hair that was falling out of a messy ponytail and oversized glasses perched on her nose. Her long, brown skirt was a little too big on her small frame, and her cream shirt had a coffee stain on it. A large, silvery gray cat slunk in at her feet, and the moment it spotted Tiki and Sherlock, it shot forward like a bullet.

"Smoke, look! Your animal friends are here," the petite woman said as Tiki let out a yip and raced toward Pat. Sherlock leaped back onto her cat tower, her hair standing on end as Smoke crouched down and stared at her, his tail twitching ominously. "It's so nice when animals get along," she said. I wondered if those oversized glasses were actually helping her see.

"Nora, you brought us books," Mildred said.

Nora glanced down as if she had forgotten she was carrying them. "Oh, yes. Someone brought these in yesterday on consignment. They're mysteries, so I wanted to bring them right over. Unless we have a case. Do we have a case yet?" Her voice was eager.

"Almost," Mildred said, taking the books. "But they hung up on Emily."

"Emily?" Nora whirled around until she spotted me, her hazel eyes blinking owlishly behind her glasses. "Emily! You're here. Tilde has said so many good things about you. Your talents were being wasted with the Duckworths. You belong here, helping us grow the number-one detective agency in Redemption."

"Here, here," Mildred said. "Not to mention, Redemption is the perfect place to find a husband." She winked at me. Inwardly, I groaned.

"And we have a case," Nora said, clasping her hands. "The flyers worked!"

"Flyers?" I asked.

"They did work," Mildred said. "But we don't have a case."

Nora's face fell. "Darn. I bet it would have been a murder case, too."

"No, I think whoever it was would have hired us to find someone who disappeared," Mildred said. "That happens a lot here. A lot more than murders."

"If you do get a case, it's probably going to be something far more mundane … like someone who thinks their spouse is cheating on them," Pat said.

"Oh, nonsense," Aunt Tilde said. "This is Redemption. We're not going to get those types of cases. There's plenty of strange and unexplained things happening here. I'm sure that's the kind of case we can expect."

"I wouldn't get my hopes up," Pat said.

"What flyers?" I asked again.

"We put flyers up around town to let everyone know about the Redemption Detective Agency," Mildred said.

"It was my idea," Nora said, clasping her hands. "They work so well on the college campuses. I was sure they would work here."

College campuses? Oh dear. I tried to keep my expression neutral. "Do you happen to have one here I can see?

"I'm sure there's one somewhere," Aunt Tilde said as she, Nora, and Mildred started pawing through desk drawers and filing cabinets.

"I remember having an extra one," Nora said.

Finally, Aunt Tilde unearthed a crumpled piece of paper, and after smoothing it out, handed it to me.

My heart sank. It definitely looked like something you would find on a college campus, and not in a good way.

It was photocopied on hot-pink paper, which drew attention to it, but also made it difficult to read the copy. Not that the copy was all that inspiring. "The Redemption Detective Agency" was written in big letters across the top. Underneath, in smaller letters was, "No case is too big or too small." Then, across the bottom, was a row of tabs with phone numbers on it.

"I thought of the 'No case is too big or too small,'" Aunt Tilde said. "I figured it covered everything."

"Hmm," I said noncommittally. Staring at the flyer was giving me an idea. "Where did you put these up?"

Mildred started ticking locations off her fingers. "The drugstore, the library, the grocery store, my beauty salon ..."

"Rocky's Pizza and the Brew House," Nora added.

"Rocky's Pizza wouldn't let us," Aunt Tilde said. "Remember?"

Nora screwed up her face. "Oh, that's right. It was the place next door to Rocky's. What is it again?"

"You're thinking of the Redemption Inn," Mildred said.

I held up a hand. "Do you remember how many you hung up?"

"Fifty," Nora said. "Or sixty."

"No, it wasn't that many," Mildred said. "Maybe thirty or forty."

"It was ten," Aunt Tilde said.

"Ten?" Nora frowned. "No, it was more than that. It had to be. We made all those copies."

"I know, and we were going to finish putting them up, but then we ran out of time because we had to get ready for Emily to arrive," Aunt Tilde said.

I wondered what exactly they had done to "get ready for me," at least here. Although maybe Aunt Tilde was also talking about the apartment.

"Do you think you can remember all the places you hung a flyer?" I asked.

"Of course," Nora said.

"Absolutely," Mildred said.

"Probably," Aunt Tilde said, although she sounded less enthused than Mildred and Nora did. "Why?"

"I have an idea," I said.

Chapter 6

I sat back in my chair, taking a short break as I stretched the kinks out of my neck.

It was Thursday morning, and the office was quiet. Mildred hadn't come in yet, and Aunt Tilde was off running "errands." I had no idea what kind; all I knew was that there were a lot of them, as she was gone for at least an hour or so nearly every day. When I asked her about them, she was notably vague.

Not that I cared about her being gone. At least then, she wasn't in my hair, and I could get things done. But the lack of a car did bother me. Aunt Tilde had told me I was welcome to her other car, an old Oldsmobile Cutlass, but we'd have to get the engine overhauled first. She was going to get it repaired, but then somehow, she ended up with the Mary Kay pink Cadillac instead.

I insisted on paying for the repairs. It felt like the least I could do. I was living rent-free in an apartment she would have no trouble finding a paying tenant for, not to mention she was also feeding me and paying all my bills. Her covering repairs on a car I would be driving felt like too much.

Of course, overhauling an engine was going to cost far more than $333, so I was going to have to wait until Geoff sent me my money. I had already called him, twice actually, to see when that would happen. He thought he could get to it next week.

Ugh.

In the meantime, I had taken a closer look at the rusted bicycle in Aunt Tilde's yard. With a little elbow grease, I figured I could make it rideable. It wasn't ideal, but it would be better than nothing.

I removed the coaster I used to cover my coffee cup and took a sip. Even though I knew it was a little silly, as I had never once seen a cockroach in the office and the idea that one would hop into my cup of coffee as it sat by my elbow seemed a little far-fetched, I still couldn't bring myself to leave it uncovered. From her cat tower, Sherlock watched me, blinking her brown eyes.

Even though the silence was nice, and I was surprised at how much work there was for a business with no clients. I still kept hoping the phone would ring with the potential client from Monday on the other end. I kept remembering the desperation in her voice, and I had a sinking feeling that she truly didn't have anywhere to turn.

On Monday, once I had seen the original flyer, I created a second one, which we then put up at all the places where the first one had been. Well, nine of them, at least. No one seemed to know where the tenth one was, although Nora had been sure Fit for Life, a local health club, had one.

"Where would they hang it?" Aunt Tilde asked. "There's no bulletin board."

"I'm sure there was one though," Nora fretted. "I can remember hanging it there."

"Maybe Tiffany removed the bulletin board," Mildred said helpfully. "We should ask her."

"I don't think that's necessary," I said quickly. "We have the new flyer up in nine locations. That should be enough." Fingers crossed. "I also created a spreadsheet with all the places where we hung one, so we can remember what we did." I showed them my clipboard with my spreadsheet.

"Oh, that's a great idea," Mildred said, peering at the clipboard.

"It's not a great idea … it's brilliant!" Aunt Tilde exclaimed, clapping her hands. "I'm so glad you're our new office manager!"

"It's only brilliant if you use it," I warned. "Will you promise me if you hang a flyer somewhere new, you'll write it down on the spreadsheet?"

Three heads solemnly nodded. Somehow, I wasn't all that convinced it would happen, but we had to start somewhere.

My idea was that, if our potential client had called us because she had seen the old flyer, maybe we could prompt her to call us a second time with the new one. But I couldn't necessarily post something like "Did you call the Redemption Detective Agency on Monday? Please call us back! We want to help you!" (Although Mildred thought that might work.) Instead, I tried to use the language the caller had used when she called. So now, the new flyer read:

"Run out of options? Nowhere to turn? Call The Redemption Detective Agency. We specialize in solving the unsolvable."

I was hesitant about solving the unsolvable part, but Aunt Tilde assured me we could stand by it. "I'm not promising we'll solve every unsolvable case, only that we specialize in it."

"Aren't we implying that we solve those cases because we specialize in them?" I asked.

"Well, then we better solve them," Aunt Tilde said. "Right?"

"Uh …" I said.

"You need to think more positively," Mildred said. "Having a man in your life will help." She winked at me.

Ugh. I made a point of busying myself with the flyer.

Once we got them photocopied (on pale-pink paper, per our compromise—I had wanted white, but Mildred kept insisting on the hot-pink) and posted, the only thing we could do was wait and hope our potential client was visiting one of the nine places we'd hung the flyer … and not the mysterious missing tenth one.

At least I had plenty to do while I waited for the phone to ring. I had calls in for an exterminator and a commercial cleaner to deal with our unwanted roommate problems. After that, I could tackle the bigger issue of how to turn a restaurant kitchen into some sort of office space. I had asked Aunt Tilde what my budget was, and she just stared at me like she didn't understand the question. "Whatever is in the bank account."

"But what about your other bills, like rent? I can't just take all your money out of the bank," I said.

"If we run out of money, I'll put more in," she said. "Just do whatever you think is best."

"But that's not how a business is supposed to run," I said. "We're not in college and checking our bank account to see how much we can spend at the bar for a wild night out."

"Then set it up like a business," she said. "I trust you. Whatever you think needs to be done."

Based on that comment, I also did some research as to private investigation licenses in Wisconsin. I discovered that yes, one is needed to operate legally. Whether or not the Redemption Detective Agency had one was still a bit of a mystery.

The phone rang. Actually, four phones rang, which reminded me to add fixing the phone system to my to-do list, so that only one phone rang, and that line could be transferred to the other phones. "The Redemption Detective Agency, Emily speaking."

There was a long pause … long enough that I almost asked if anyone was there. I was sure I could hear breathing, though, so I stayed silent.

"Can you really solve unsolvable cases?"

I sat up straighter. It was the woman from Monday. I was sure of it. "It's what we focus on." I felt like I was skirting around the truth a bit, but I didn't want her to hang up again. "What's going on? What do you need help with?"

There was another long pause. "It's my son. I'm just … I don't know what to do. No one believes me. I know he didn't do it, but I don't know how to prove it, and time is running out for his appeal …"

"Hold on," I said. I was busy taking notes as fast as I could. "Did you say appeal?"

"Yes, his appeal. He's in jail right now for a crime he didn't commit."

Oh boy. This was way above our heads. I was almost afraid to ask the next question. "What was the crime?"

"It was murder, but I know he didn't do it."

I dropped the pen. There was no way we could take on this case. I opened my mouth to tell her so, but she kept talking.

"I have nowhere else to turn. I know calling you is a long shot, but I don't know what else to do."

"Have you hired private detectives in the past?" Maybe I could encourage her to hire a different agency, preferably one that was licensed.

She let out a laugh that was devoid of humor. "The first one I hired told me there was nothing to find; said my son was guilty, and the best thing I could do was learn to accept it. This was after I paid them their full fee, mind you. The second one told me it was a lost cause, as well, but at least they didn't take my money to tell me that. The third never returned my call."

Well, that didn't sound good. If those agencies couldn't find any evidence to exonerate her son, I didn't see how we were going to do much better. But even though I knew I should probably tell her that, the desperation in her voice kept stopping me from saying it. "How did you find out about us?" I asked instead. If nothing else, maybe I could at least do some market research.

There was a snort. "I've known Tilde for years. When I heard she was opening up a detective agency, I was … skeptical. But then I heard that Tilde had assisted Charlie Kingsley with a couple of cases, and I thought well, maybe she could help after all. And then, when I saw the flyer for the Redemption Detective Agency, it felt like a sign." Her voice shifted. "You put out a new flyer after I called, didn't you?"

I hesitated, but it seemed silly to try and hide from the truth. "I did."

"Why?"

The question took me aback, but after a few minutes of frantically sorting through possible answers, I found myself settling on the truth. "I just … I wanted to help you. I could hear how much you needed help, and I was hoping you would call back."

She was quiet for a moment. "So, can you?"

My heart twisted in my chest. In her voice, I could hear not just desperation, but desperate hope.

I really needed to tell her no. It would be cruel to get her hopes up only to discover we weren't able to solve the unsolvable after all.

But I could hear Tilde's voice in my head, as clear as if she was standing next to me, saying the words. *Well, then, we better solve them.*

"Why don't you come in, and let's see what we can do," I said.

Chapter 7

"A client! This is so exciting," Mildred said as she arranged a vase of fresh flowers next to the water jug. "And a murder case, at that!"

"Emily is definitely our lucky charm," Aunt Tilde said, flashing a quick smile in my direction as she made a fresh pot of coffee.

I forced a smile back, although inwardly, I was having serious second thoughts. Maybe I should have told Greta that we couldn't help her. What right did I have to get her hopes up only to dash them? But then I reminded myself that she actually knew Aunt Tilde, so if nothing else, this could be like a couple of old friends getting together for a chat.

And it wasn't like I lied to her. I told her she should come in to discuss all the options, and that was exactly what we were doing.

But I couldn't shake the uncomfortable feeling I had.

When I told Aunt Tilde our new client's name was Greta, she knew immediately who I was talking about. "Oh, that was a dreadful case. Happened a few years ago."

"What happened, exactly?"

Aunt Tilde frowned. "A fight gone wrong or something. Nasty business. I can't recall all the details. We should probably just wait for Greta to arrive. I don't want to tell you something wrong."

Even though I didn't like not having any details to prepare myself for the meeting, I couldn't argue with that logic.

The bell on the door tinkled its little welcoming tune, and a woman walked in. She looked old and worn out, with short, gray hair and tired, watery, blue eyes.

"Greta," Aunt Tilde said, hurrying forward to take her hands. "I'm so glad you came in."

Greta gave her a faint smile. "It's nice to see you, too." She glanced over her shoulder. "Oh, hi Mildred. I didn't expect to see you here. Are you a client as well?"

"Actually, I'm a detective," Mildred said.

"You're a detective?" Greta seemed to turn green, like she might be sick, and I wondered if she was about to bolt.

"And you've met Emily," Aunt Tilde interrupted, gesturing toward me. I smiled weakly. "She's my niece."

"Oh, yes, we've met." Greta nodded toward me.

"Come, sit." Aunt Tilde waved her forward. "I want to hear all the details."

For a moment, Greta didn't move, and I could almost see the wheels turning in her head, evaluating whether she should stay or go. Was she really going to put her faith in a detective agency where the two detectives were a retired nurse and a retired teacher? And she hadn't even met Nora yet. I almost felt a little sorry for her.

"Coffee?" Mildred asked brightly, holding up a mug.

Greta jerked her head to look at Mildred, while she took a small step back.

I leaped to my feet. "I know we're a little … unorthodox," I said. "But that's part of what makes us different. We're not like the police or other detectives who have been trained in the same way, so they tend to approach cases in a similar fashion. We have a different approach, and that's what makes us unique. Obviously, the choice is yours, but why not sit down and see if we can help you or not?"

Greta stared at me. Actually, all three women were staring at me, but Aunt Tilde and Mildred beamed, like I was their prized student who just aced an exam.

"I guess it wouldn't hurt to chat," Greta said finally.

"Great," Aunt Tilde said, leading her to a chair by one of the desks. I dragged over two more chairs, as well as a notebook and pen to take notes, as Mildred brought over a cup of coffee.

"So," Aunt Tilde said once we were all settled in. "What's going on?"

Greta circled the cup of coffee in her palms, but didn't taste it. "It's about Hal. My son. My only son." Her voice caught at the end, but her expression didn't change.

Aunt Tilde's face was grave as she reached out to squeeze Greta's knee. "I know. I remember the case, but it might be helpful for all of us if you start at the beginning."

Greta nodded and took a deep breath. "It happened almost four years ago. Hal was a student at the University of Riverview. A senior. He had his whole life in front of him." She swallowed hard. "It was April, a couple of weeks after spring break. He was at a party when Rocco, one of his friends, was killed."

"Wait, a college senior killed at a party? I remember that story," I said, although the memories were hazy. "But I thought the person who killed him confessed."

Greta's face seemed to collapse on itself. "He did. My son confessed to a murder he didn't commit." She lifted one hand and covered her face.

I met Aunt Tilde's eyes and saw my own misgivings reflected there. No wonder why no one took her case. How on Earth could we possibly "solve" a murder when the murderer already confessed?

"Why don't you tell us what happened at the party?" Aunt Tilde asked gently. "Or at least what you think happened?"

Greta scrubbed at her face before dropping her hand. "He had been friends with Rocco for years. They were roommates freshman year and immediately clicked. Why would Hal kill his best friend? It makes no sense. Besides, I know my son. He's no killer."

"Do you know what happened at the party?" I asked, hoping that would be enough to get her back on track.

Greta took a deep breath. "I don't know all the details, but I do know he and Rocco had been having some ... issues, I guess, a few months before Rocco's death. Usually, when Hal would call, he would tell me all about what he and Rocco were doing, but something shifted during those few months, and he stopped talking about Rocco. When I asked about him, he would say Rocco was fine, but that was it. Nothing more. I even asked him once if he and Rocco were having a fight, but he said no, it wasn't anything like that. I thought maybe their friendship was just naturally coming to an end because they were both graduating and about to start living different lives. Hal was planning to stay in the area, either Riverview or back home to Redemption, but Rocco was likely moving to a bigger city. Maybe Chicago or New York."

Neither Mildred, Aunt Tilde, nor I said anything, but I suspected we were all thinking the same thing. That tracked from what I remembered of the case.

It also did exactly the opposite of exonerating her son.

"So, were they drifting apart, or was there something else going on?" Aunt Tilde pressed.

Greta shifted uncomfortably in her chair. "Something did happen between them. I'm just not sure what it was. Hal refuses to tell me. But it couldn't have been that bad … they remained roommates and still went to parties together. They even went on ski trips and their annual spring break vacation. So, how could it be that terrible?" She turned and looked at all of us defiantly, as if daring us to question her son's relationship with the man he confessed to murdering.

"Back to the night of the party," I said, feeling like I was going to need to push her if I wanted a straight answer out of her. "I remember hearing something about them fighting. Was that true?"

Greta dropped her gaze to her feet, which she had started shuffling back and forth. "That's what he said. They had gotten into a huge fight earlier in the day, and between that and the alcohol…" she let out a deep, long sigh. "He said it was an accident. He didn't mean to do it."

"He … uh… hit Rocco on the head with something, right?" I asked.

She nodded sadly. "At first, it was ruled an accident. Rocco had plenty to drink that night, and the police just assumed he had fallen and hit his head. A freak accident. Those things happen. But when they looked a little more closely and realized the angle at which he was hit, how he had fallen didn't match up. And that meant someone hit him. The police investigated, and, well, Hal confessed."

Greta paused again, still staring at her feet. The rest of us didn't say anything either. I was wondering if they were thinking the same thing I was … that there was just nothing we could do to help her.

"Why do you think Hal is innocent?" Aunt Tilde asked.

Greta snapped her head up. "He's my son. I know my son,

and he's not a killer. I don't care how much alcohol he drank that night." Her tone was fierce.

"I agree," Mildred said. All three of us turned to stare at her. She had been so quiet, I had forgotten about her. She looked faintly surprised by our attention. "He was one of my students," she explained. "I remember him well. He was a nice boy. I don't see him growing up to be a killer." She made a face as she sipped her coffee. "Not like some of my students. I could tell you stories ..."

"Other than that," Aunt Tilde cut in, sending a sharp look to Mildred, who sipped more of her coffee. "I remember him, too, and I agree, he never struck me as someone who would be in jail for killing someone. But if we're going to prove he didn't do it, we're going to need a little more to go on."

Greta's shoulders slumped. "That's what all the other private detectives said. The fact that he confessed ... there's really not much they can do. But I know in my heart he's not guilty. There has to be something we can do to help him, right?" She looked at all three of us with such naked, desperate hope on her face, it made my heart hurt.

"Do you know why he confessed?" I asked. "Especially if he didn't do it, I mean. There has to be a reason he would confess to a crime he didn't commit."

One of her hands balled up in a fist. "I don't know. He wouldn't tell me."

She's lying. The thought instantly shot through my head like an arrow. But what was she lying about? That he did actually tell her? But why wouldn't she tell us what he said?

Unless it made him look even more guilty.

"Well, if we're going to help you, we're going to need to know," Aunt Tilde said.

What? I nearly fell out of my chair. Aunt Tilde couldn't possibly have just said we were going to take this case.

Greta looked at Aunt Tilde, her expression a mixed combination of joy and suspicion. "You think you can help?"

"We can certainly try," Aunt Tilde said. "After all, that's what we're all about. Solving the unsolvable."

What about cases that are already solved, just not in the way the client wants? I kept my lips pressed tightly closed, so the words wouldn't slip out.

"What ..." Greta paused, and her cheeks flushed red. "This is so embarrassing. I should have started with this. How much is this going to cost me, and is there any way to work out a payment plan? I'm completely broke right now, and time is of the essence, because we're trying to get a new trial, even though his lawyer hasn't done a thing other than cash my checks. I don't know what I'm going to do ..."

Aunt Tilde put a hand on Greta's arm. "It's fine. We'll do it for free."

I dropped my pen. Not only were we taking a case we couldn't possibly solve, but we were doing it for free? What was Aunt Tilde thinking? She was going to go broke with this so-called detective agency.

Greta seemed equally floored. "No, I couldn't possibly ask you to do that. I have to pay you something."

Aunt Tilde waved a hand. "Nonsense. This is why I started this agency. Because I want to help people who need help, no matter their financial circumstances."

"Exactly," Mildred said, nodding her head. Obviously, I was going to have to sit both of them down and explain what it meant to own a business.

"I'm not looking for a handout," Greta said, but the tension in her shoulders had immediately eased.

"Of course you aren't," Aunt Tilde said.

"And it's just so frustrating, because part of the reason why I don't have the money to pay you is because of this lawyer, but he doesn't seem to be doing anything to help Hal. So, I have no choice but to hire a private detective," Greta said.

Aunt Tilde tapped her finger against her lips. "I think I may have a solution to your attorney problem."

Greta's eyes went wide. "Really? That would be such a lifesaver."

"I can't promise anything, as I have to make a few calls, but I'll get back to you," Aunt Tilde said.

I squeezed my eyes closed. *Please Lord, don't let her "solution" be calling Dmitry to break the attorney's legs.*

"In the meantime," Aunt Tilde continued. "I'm going to need as much information as you can give me. No detail is too small."

"I can give you a list of Hal and Rocco's friends who were at the party," Greta said. "You can talk to them."

"Didn't, uh, the police already interview them?" I asked.

Greta made a face. "I doubt it. Or if they did, they didn't do a good job. They railroaded my son from the beginning."

A confession will do that, I wanted to say, but I kept my mouth clamped shut. Instead, I turned to a fresh sheet of paper to take down the friends' names.

"Rocco's girlfriend was there, too," Greta said. "Fern is her name. She and Hal were friends, as well. If anyone would know what was going on between those two, it would be Fern."

I dutifully jotted down Fern's first and last name as Greta rattled them off.

"What about your son?" Aunt Tilde asked. "Can you set it up so we can interview him?"

"I'll need to make a few calls, but yes, I'm sure I can," Greta said. "Anything else?"

"Do you have the police report? That would be helpful," Aunt Tilde said.

"What about his things?" Mildred asked. "Like any planners or notebooks where he might have written things down during that time."

"I've got all of his belongings," Greta said. "They're boxed up. You can go through whatever you want. I also have the file from the first private detective agency I hired, which I think has a copy of the police report. You can have it all."

"That would be great," Aunt Tilde said.

"Do you want me to get it now?" Greta asked, standing up. She was still holding the full cup of coffee and awkwardly looked around for a place to set it. I swooped in and took it from her.

"We'll call you tomorrow to arrange a pickup," Aunt Tilde said. "And hopefully, I'll have a solution for your attorney problem by then, as well."

"That would be incredible," Greta started to say just as the bell on the door tinkled, and Nora rushed in, along with Smoke. Her hair seemed frizzier than normal, and her glasses were askew. Greta was staring at her with something like horror on her face.

"Am I late?" she asked as she straightened her glasses. Smoke made a beeline for Sherlock, who immediately started hissing.

Aunt Tilde beamed at her. "Nora, meet our new client, Greta."

Nora hurriedly adjusted her glasses again as she peered at her. "Are you the one we wrote the flyer for?"

Greta swallowed hard, and I wondered if she was back to rethinking hiring the Redemption Detective Agency after all. But then she seemed to remember that she wasn't actually paying for any of this, and she forced a small smile on her face as she shook Nora's hand.

I could only hope this wasn't going to turn into a bigger disaster than it already was.

Chapter 8

"Have you lost your mind?" I asked as Aunt Tilde hung up the phone. Greta had already left, and Mildred was cleaning up as Nora tried to coax Smoke away from Sherlock.

"What are you talking about?" Aunt Tilde asked as she dug around in her purse. "Where are my keys?"

"We can't take on this client," I said.

Nora blinked owlishly at me. "Why? What's wrong with this client?"

"She's not a client. That's what's wrong," I said.

"Of course she's a client," Mildred said. "She just said she was."

"But that doesn't make her one," I said through my teeth.

Nora adjusted her glasses. "I don't understand."

"Emily is just tired and confused," Mildred said. "She's been working too hard and needs to go out on a date."

"Where are my keys?" Aunt Tilde asked again, pulling open the desk drawers. "Has anyone seen them?"

"I am not tired and confused," I said, trying to keep from screaming. "I'm stating a fact. She's not our client for two reasons. One, she's not paying us."

"You heard her. Her lawyer is bleeding her dry. We can't charge her," Aunt Tilde said.

"We are a *business*. And by its very definition, we are supposed to get paid for the services we offer," I said.

Nora frowned. "She does have a point. We probably should charge something for investigating a case. Right?"

"Maybe she'll give us a tip," Mildred said. "Once we solve the case."

"And that leads me to my second point," I said, deciding to ignore the tip comment and refrain from pointing out how businesses don't survive on tips alone. "She can't be a client because there's no case. Her son confessed. The case is solved. There's nothing more to be done."

"Hal didn't kill anyone," Mildred said. "I had that boy in my classroom for an entire year. He wouldn't hurt a fly."

"But he *confessed* to killing his friend," I said.

"It was obviously some kind of misunderstanding," Mildred said.

"Exactly," Aunt Tilde said as she widened her search for her keys to the coffee-maker area. "Hence, why Greta *is* a client."

I couldn't believe I was having this argument. "He's in jail. Why would he confess to a crime he didn't commit and go to jail for it?"

"Well, that's what we have to figure out," Aunt Tilde said, looking around the water jug. "Tada! Finally." She held up her keys triumphantly. "Emily, let's go."

"Go? Where are we going?" I was feeling very grumpy with everyone associated with the Redemption Detective Agency, especially Aunt Tilde. The last thing I felt like doing was getting into a car with her.

She rattled her keys at me. "To solve Greta's lawyer problem. Come on, we need to go."

Mildred perked up. "I'll come too. Where are *my* keys?" She frowned as she looked around.

Nora sighed. "I better stay here in case another client comes in." That thought seemed to perk her up.

Aunt Tilde started moving toward the door. "Emily, let's go."

For a moment, I thought about refusing. Really, it was the last thing I wanted to do. But I also didn't particularly want to stay in the office with Nora and Smoke. Smoke had been giving me the evil eye, and I had a feeling the only reason he hadn't attacked me yet was because he was more interested in torturing Sherlock. Plus, if her way of solving Greta's attorney problem was doing something borderline illegal, I probably needed to be there to talk her out of it.

"Fine," I muttered as I made my way toward the door. "Don't think this conversation is over though."

She beamed at me. "I wouldn't dream of it."

***

Aunt Tilde didn't want to wait for Mildred to get organized enough to drive her own car, so she came with us. She sat in the front seat while I was relegated to the back, which meant I couldn't have the conversation I really wanted to have with my aunt. I sat in stony silence, fuming to myself as Mildred and Aunt Tilde bickered about who was going to get to do what. "I should be the one to go through Hal's belongings," Mildred said.

"That's something we should both do," Aunt Tilde said. "We don't want to miss a clue."

"What if there's something ... inappropriate in there?" Mildred said. "We don't want to embarrass the poor boy by all of us seeing it."

"What makes you think you should be the only one to see it?" Aunt Tilde retorted.

Mildred straightened herself up. "I was his teacher."

I closed my eyes. I definitely needed my own car. If I didn't hear from Geoff by Monday, I was calling him again.

"Here we go," Aunt Tilde said, pulling into a parking spot in front of a squat building filled with office suites.

Mildred stared at the building. "Wait. What are we doing here?"

Aunt Tilde unbuckled her seatbelt. "I told you, we're solving Greta's lawyer problem."

Mildred looked at her in shock. "Oh no. This isn't a good idea."

"Do you have a better one?" Aunt Tilde shot back, opening the door.

Visions of Dmitry danced in my head. "What's going on? What's not a good idea?"

Mildred pressed her lips together. "Getting *him* involved."

Oh no. This definitely wasn't good. "Who?"

"He's not that bad," Aunt Tilde argued.

"You didn't have him as a student," Mildred said.

Well, that probably ruled out Dmitry, but I wasn't sure if that was good or bad, at this point. "*Who?*"

"Nick Stewart," Mildred said, gritting her teeth.

Nick Stewart. That didn't sound like the name of a leg-breaker.

"Who is he?"

"Trouble," Mildred said darkly.

"Do you have a better idea?" Aunt Tilde demanded.

Mildred looked between her and the building, then unbuckled her seatbelt. "Fine. But if this doesn't work, it's your fault."

"Noted," Aunt Tilde said, opening the car door. "Let's go. He's expecting us."

I slid out of the back, following Mildred and Aunt Tilde as they crossed the parking lot while wondering just how bad someone would have to be for Mildred to object.

Did he work for the mob? Was he a hit man?

Aunt Tilde headed for a door with a small sign that read "Stewart and Affiliates."

"Who are the affiliates?" I asked, but before anyone could answer me, Aunt Tilde was opening the door and ushering us inside.

We were standing in a small reception room with a couch and an empty receptionist's desk. The colors were all beige and brown, as dull as it could possibly get. There was another door that was partially open in the back. "Just a minute," a male voice rang out.

"It's not too late to leave," Mildred hissed.

"Give me another idea, and we'll go right now," Aunt Tilde hissed back.

Mildred stuck a tongue out at her as Aunt Tilde glared right back.

The door flew open. "Sorry about that. Client call and my assistant is out this week."

I blinked. The man standing there was disheveled, with his pale-blue shirt unbuttoned at the top and his tie loosened around his neck. His black hair was rumpled, like he had been running his fingers through it, and a five o'clock shadow covered his face.

I couldn't help but compare him to Geoff, who was always clean shaven, and whose shirt was always buttoned up and tie in place. Even at home, when he changed into "casual" clothes, they were always crisp and pressed and suited his classically handsome features.

This man, on the other hand, seemed to exude danger like a

fine cologne. He looked like a rougher version of Tom Cruise. The tie and pressed shirt confused me a bit. Did people who broke legs for a living wear ties? Maybe he wasn't the person who actually beat people up, but rather the one who ordered others to do it.

"No problem, Nick. I'm glad you could see us with such short notice," Aunt Tilde said.

"I hope you're keeping yourself out of trouble," Mildred said, her tone like ice.

Nick focused his startling green eyes on her and seemed to straighten up. "Ms. Schmidt. I didn't expect you." He ran a hand through his hair, probably to try and smooth it out, but he just ended up making it more tousled than before.

"I didn't expect to be here either, but ..." Mildred eyed Aunt Tilde. "Tilde thinks you can help." Her tone made it clear she disagreed with that sentiment.

Nick flashed her a grin that made my heart stutter in my chest. "You know me. I'm happy to help whenever I can."

"Just make sure you actually help rather than making the situation worse," Mildred said meaningfully as she gave him a stern look.

Nick swallowed hard, then turned to me. "And who might this be?" He flashed that smile again, but I kept my expression neutral and tried to ignore the fluttering in my chest.

"That's my niece, Emily," Aunt Tilde.

"She's off-limits," Mildred said. "She's already dating someone."

"I am not," I said before I could stop myself.

"Well, you will be," Mildred said. "Jerome is a fine man ... a catch for any woman."

Nick watched the exchange, a bemused expression on his face. Part of me suddenly wanted to wipe that smirk off his face.

"Anyway," Aunt Tilde said hastily. "We should probably get down to business, as I'm sure Nick has a busy schedule. Right, Nick?"

"Yes, ma'am," Nick said, taking a step back with a flourish. "Come on in, and let's discuss what I can do for you."

We all shuffled into his office, which was an absolute disaster. Piles of paper and files were scattered everywhere—on his desk, on top of the filing cabinets behind his desk, on one of the chairs in front of his desk. He quickly scooped that pile up and placed it on the floor. He offered the two chairs to Mildred and Aunt Tilde, then pulled his office chair around and gestured for me to sit in it.

"Where are you going to sit?" I asked, feeling a little uncomfortable taking his chair.

He pushed aside a towering stack of files on his desk, which amazingly did not tip over, and perched himself on the edge while waving again at the chair.

I carefully picked my way over, keeping my hands firmly at my sides even though they were twitching to tidy up. It smelled like coffee, leather, and old books.

"So, how can I help?" He asked, fishing a yellow legal pad and pen out of the chaos on his desk. He angled his head toward me. "I'm assuming you're the person I'm supposed to be helping."

I nearly choked. Why did I think it was a good idea to live with Aunt Tilde? I should have stayed in Riverview and lived on my sister's couch. "Wait, you told him too?" I demanded.

"What? No, that's not ... I ..." Aunt Tilde sputtered, looking as shocked as I felt.

I didn't let her finish. "Who didn't you tell about the Duckworths?"

"The Duckworths?" Nick's jaw dropped in surprise. "That's the case?" His expression sharpened, and his smile turned wolfish. "You have my attention."

"You can take that attention and point it elsewhere," I retorted. "I'm not the one who needs help."

Nick's eyes gleamed as he studied me. "I do love a challenge," he mused.

"I told you, she's taken," Mildred snapped.

He held his hands up. "I'm just trying to figure out how you'd like me to help, that's all."

"It's our new client," Aunt Tilde said quickly. "She needs a new attorney for her son. Can you represent him?"

"Hold on," I blurted, holding up my hand. "You're a lawyer?"

The three of them all turned their heads to stare at me. "Of course," Aunt Tilde said. "Who else is going to help Greta?"

"Well … I …" I wasn't sure what to say. My earlier thoughts about him being some sort of hired muscle now seemed rather foolish, especially when the more I thought about it, the more obvious it became I was sitting in the middle of a messy lawyer's office.

"What did you think I am?" Nick asked, his voice amused.

"Your sign doesn't say you're a lawyer," I said, which didn't precisely answer the question. "It just says Stewart and Associates."

"That's because at one time, there was an associate, but things change." While his voice was civil, his eyes were cold. A shiver ran up my spine. Even if Nick wasn't in the leg-breaking business, he clearly wasn't someone to mess with.

"Nick is one of the best lawyers in Redemption," Aunt Tilde said with just a hint of pride in her voice. "Any lawyer would be lucky to work with him."

Nick blinked, and some of the warmth came back into his face. "Flattery will get you everywhere," he teased. "Although, I will admit, I'm getting a little worried about this new client. Why does she need a new lawyer?"

"Because her son's current lawyer isn't doing anything but taking money from her," Aunt Tilde said.

Nick tapped his pen against his pad. "If the lawyer isn't doing anything, why hasn't she fired him or her yet?"

"Because she needs someone to handle getting him another trial …" Aunt Tilde began.

Nick's eyes widened. "*Another* trial? Her son was already convicted?"

"*Wrongfully* convicted," Aunt Tilde said. "That's why he needs another trial. Because he was railroaded."

His gaze narrowed. "And I assume that's why you're involved? To find the real culprit?"

"Exactly," Aunt Tilde said. "Greta needs all the help she can get."

"Greta?" Nick gave her a careful look. "What exactly is her son convicted of?"

"Well, murder, but again, he's innocent," Aunt Tilde said.

Nick pinched his nose. "This is the Jarrett case, isn't it? The one where he confessed to killing his friend?"

"But he didn't do it," Aunt Tilde insisted.

Nick sighed. "You do understand there's a confession, right?"

"Yes, but there could be a lot of reasons for that," Aunt Tilde said.

"Like he could be guilty," I muttered under my breath. At least I thought it was under my breath, but both Nick and Aunt Tilde shot me looks. Nick's look was amused, while Aunt Tilde's was the opposite.

"He could have been coerced," she insisted, glaring at me.

"Possible," Nick said. "And if he was, that would certainly warrant a new trial. *Was* he coerced?"

"Um… I don't actually know," Aunt Tilde said.

"Do you know the current standing of their request for a new trial?" Nick asked.

Aunt Tilde squirmed in her chair. "Not exactly."

Nick tapped his pen on the pad. "I'm not going to lie to you. It's not easy getting a new trial even under the best of circumstances. Having a confession makes things extremely difficult."

"So why does he have an attorney trying to get a new trial if it's so impossible?" Mildred asked. "The attorney must know something we don't, right?"

"Maybe that's why the attorney isn't doing anything other than taking her money," I said.

Nick pointed at me with his pen. "Now that might be something I could help with. If her attorney is billing her for unethical or fraudulent reasons, there might be something there."

"Does that mean you'll take the case?" Aunt Tilde asked.

Nick hesitated. "I would need to know more," he said finally. "I don't want to make her any false promises. But I could at least look into it and give you my professional opinion."

Aunt Tilde clapped her hands together. "Oh, that's wonderful! I can't wait to tell Greta."

He clicked his pen. "Great. I'll need as many details as possible, but we can start with whatever basics you have. I won't charge her to initially look into it, but I'm assuming if I take the case, I should work out the financial details directly with Greta." He paused, and when Aunt Tilde didn't say anything, glanced up and raised an eyebrow at her.

She sighed. "There is, um, one other little ... well ... detail I should probably mention."

Nick clicked his pen again. "Oh?"

She shifted in her seat. "She doesn't have any money. That's part of the reason why I wanted to get you involved. That lawyer took it all and isn't doing anything to get her son out of jail."

Nick leaned back, at least as far as he could while still balancing on the edge of his desk, and folded his arms across his chest. "Are you asking me to do this pro bono?"

Aunt Tilde twisted her hands in her lap. "I know, I know. I wouldn't ask, but she's desperate. She has nowhere else to turn."

"If it helps, we're not taking any money either," I said. I wasn't exactly sure why Aunt Tilde was so determined to take on a client and case we couldn't solve, let alone drag someone else into it, but if it meant so much to her, I was willing to do whatever I could to make it happen.

Hopefully, once she got this case out of her system, she would be more likely to accept others that we not only had a reasonably decent shot of solving, but that would pay us, too.

Nick was studying me, those dark-green eyes intent. I could feel the heat rise up in my chest and neck even as told myself I was being ridiculous. I had no interest in dating anyone, much less another lawyer, and especially not one who couldn't even be bothered to keep his office neat and organized.

"I'll do it," he said abruptly.

"Yes!" Aunt Tilde shouted, dancing a little in her seat. "I knew you wouldn't let her down."

Nick held up a hand. "At least, I'll look into it, and if I find something I can help with, I'll do it pro bono. But only if I find something."

"Of course, of course," Aunt Tilde said airily, waving her hand. "Greta is going to be so thrilled when she finds out."

"Hmm," Mildred said. She didn't look nearly as excited as Aunt Tilde did. She shook her finger at Nick. "Just remember you're doing a job. That's it. Don't get any other ideas."

"I wouldn't dream of it," Nick said solemnly.

Chapter 9

I yanked another weed out of the garden, wishing I could yank Nick's smirking face out of my head.

It was Saturday afternoon, and I had spent most of the day in the garden, taking out my frustrations on any plant growing where it didn't belong.

It wasn't just Nick that was annoying me, although if I was being honest, that was probably the majority of it. It was all my life choices that had led to me living in the strange little town of Redemption with my eccentric aunt and working at her completely unsustainable business. Not to mention I had no car and no money, and no way to make any money. After all, how could I possibly draw a paycheck from a business that had no income? It was bad enough I was living in her apartment and eating her food. At this rate, I was never going to be able to work my way out of the disaster that had become my life.

Hopefully, Geoff would honor his word and send me my money in the next few days. If I had it, I wouldn't necessarily need to stay. If I wanted, I could go back to Riverview and stay with my sister while I looked for an actual job. Even if I was locked out of jobs in my field, I was sure I could land something with a legit business that had an actual income stream.

Sweat mixed with dirt was dripping into my eyes, so I paused to wipe it away and stretch my back.

Which was when I saw the dog again.

He was closer than the last time, hovering next to the water dish I had faithfully refilled each day. It was now empty, and he was staring at me as he panted, his tongue lolling out.

"You probably want some water," I said as I went to fetch the hose. The dog licked his chops as he carefully watched me. I was no longer afraid of him. Mostly, I just felt sorry for him. I did what

I could, keeping his water dish full throughout the week, and even calling both the humane society and animal control to see if they could help. The humane society told me I would have to bring the dog in myself or call animal control. Animal control took down the information and said they would patrol the area, but either they weren't looking that hard, or the dog didn't want to be found.

He started lapping up the water the moment I stepped away after filling his dish. I watched him for a few moments. Definitely too thin. I could see his ribs poking out from under his filthy coat. I figured I should maybe start feeding him, as well, at least until I figured out how to get him some real help.

I left the dog to his water and went back to my weeding and pruning. I was close to having the entire garden cleaned up, at which point I was going to start on the shrubs and trees that bordered the yard. Although maybe mowing the lawn should come first …

"Emily! What did you do?"

Aunt Tilde's voice startled me so much, I fell over backwards. The dog, who had been lying down in the shade, leaped to his feet and shot her a suspicious look.

"What? What?" I looked around frantically. Had I broken something and not realized it? Had I accidentally pulled up a rose bush instead of a weed?

Aunt Tilde was staring at the dog like she had seen a ghost. In one hand, she held a bowl full of what looked like cat food, and in the other, a cordless phone. "The dog. How did you get him to stay here?"

I glanced between her and the dog, who had taken a couple of steps backward. "I don't know. I just gave him water."

She gaped at me. "Water? That's it?"

"Yeah, water." I slapped a bug away from the back of my neck. "Should I not have done that?"

She shook her head, making her frizzy hair fly around her face. "No, it's not that. I've been trying to get that poor dog to trust me for weeks now. See?" She shook the bowl with the cat food. "I've even been feeding him, but he still won't trust me."

I peered into the bowl. "Maybe it's the food you're feeding him.

What is that?"

"Cat food."

I glanced at the dog. He was still standing in the same spot as he watched us. "Should you be giving a dog cat food?"

"I don't have anything else, and the poor dear needs something. Look how thin he is." She gestured with her arm.

I agreed with her.

"Here." She thrust the dish toward me. "You feed him."

"Me?" While I didn't think he was going to attack me, at least I was pretty sure he wouldn't, I still wasn't sure how comfortable I was approaching him with food. "Why don't you do it?"

"Because he doesn't trust me," she said matter-of-factly.

I looked down at the food dish and then at the dog, who licked his chops. "I don't know how much he trusts me either. I just give him water."

"He trusts you," she said as she nudged me with her shoulder. "Go on. That poor dog needs to be fed. Just like he needs a good home."

She wasn't wrong about that.

I took a deep breath and looked at the dog, who cocked his head. Gingerly, I took a step forward. He didn't move. I took another step.

"See, it's fine," Aunt Tilde called out from behind me. "I told you he likes you."

"Yeah, he likes me just fine until he decides to take my arm off," I muttered as I kept slowly walking toward him. The dog grinned at me.

I waited until I almost reached his water dish before I put the food down and backed up a few steps. The dog waited until I was a few steps away before giving me a quick wag of his tail and coming forward to sniff the food.

"See? Look at that," Aunt Tilde crowed as the dog began eating. "I told you he likes you."

"We should be feeding him dog food, not cat food," I said.

"I can go get some," she said. "Along with a leash and a collar."

I whirled around. "Why would you buy a leash and collar?"

She looked at me like I was missing the obvious. "How else are we going to catch him? That dog doesn't deserve to be a stray. He should have a home."

I turned back around to watch the dog, who was still eating. "Maybe we should call animal control and let them pick him up."

"It's Saturday afternoon, I'm sure they're closed until Monday. And once Monday comes, then what? If we don't catch him now, animal control might not be able to find him on Monday."

"What about the humane society?" Although even as I said it, I knew I'd need something, like a collar and leash, to bring him in.

"They're not open until Monday either," Aunt Tilde said. "Honestly, I think the best thing we can do for that sweet dog is keep him safe and fed until Monday."

I frowned as I eyed the dog. What she said was true. Someone needed to take care of him until Monday.

But that someone didn't need to be us. Especially me. I wasn't good with dogs anyway.

The dog lifted his head from the bowl and gave me a tentative tail wag.

"See? He likes you," Aunt Tilde said.

I sighed. "He needs a bath. Look how filthy he is."

"I can pick up dog shampoo and a brush, too."

"He probably has fleas."

"I'll get flea medicine."

Ugh. I could feel my defenses cracking. Still, that didn't mean I had to agree to spending my Saturday night giving a stray dog a bath. "Maybe we just … stick him in the garage," I said. "At least until Monday. That would probably work, right?"

Aunt Tilde made a face. "It could. It's kind of hot in there, though. Plus, there might be chemicals or other things he could get into. But we could probably make it work. Especially since you have other plans."

I looked at her in surprise. "Plans? What are you talking about? What plans?"

"Oh! I think I forgot to tell you." She waved her hand holding the phone. "This was the other reason why I came out here. Mildred called."

I was instantly suspicious. "What did she want?"

Aunt Tilde's expression was full of innocence. "Oh, she was wondering if you wanted to go over to her house for dinner. She thought it might be a nice change from hanging out here with your old aunt." She rubbed her hands on her bright-green shorts. "Also, she said if that sounded good, you should wear something nice. A dress maybe. If you have one, that is."

I squeezed my hands into fists. I couldn't believe this. Did she really think I was that stupid? "What did you tell her?"

"That I would have to ask you and call her back." Aunt Tilde looked up and squinted at the sun. "Anyway, I better get going if I'm going to make it to the pet store before they close and before you need to be at Mildred's."

"Why are you going to the pet store if we're going to put him in the garage?" I asked.

"We still need a leash and collar, right? And dog food. We should at least try to fatten him up before Monday." She waved the phone as she started moving toward the house. "I can call Mildred before I leave. What do you want me to tell her?"

I glanced over to the dog, who had sidled closer to me ... so close, I could almost reach out and pet him if I wanted. His eyes were a soft brown, and he stared into mine with such a hopeful, trusting expression.

"Tell her that I need to take care of a dog tonight," I said. "And pick up some shampoo and flea medicine while you're at it."

Aunt Tilde gave me a solemn nod. "On it."

***

She picked up a lot more than the items I'd requested. She came home with a brush, dog conditioner (to make it easier to brush out the knots), a dog bed, treats, a long line to tie him up in the backyard, and even a couple of toys. "They're so cute," she said. "I couldn't help myself."

"But we're not going to keep him," I said, alarmed.

"Don't worry, we'll just donate them," she said as she patted my arm.

That didn't make me feel any better, but I couldn't put my finger on why.

The dog, for his part, was a very good boy throughout his bath, brushing, and flea treatment, even though it took several hours and left me and Aunt Tilde soaking wet. When he was done, he looked and smelled much better. After removing all the filth, it was clear he was a yellow lab ... or at the very least, a yellow lab mix.

Aunt Tilde also talked me into keeping him in my apartment. "I thought we agreed he would stay in the garage," I protested.

"Oh, we can't have him in there," she said. "There're all sorts of nasty things, like oil and antifreeze. Besides, it's too hot for him."

"But he can't be in my apartment. What if he has fleas or bugs?" I didn't want a dog in my living space. I liked having a nice, clean, orderly home to return to.

She looked at me bemusedly. "Honey, you just washed him. Three times. He's cleaner than I am."

"He'll shed."

"That's what vacuum cleaners are for," Aunt Tilde said.

"What if he isn't housebroken?" This was a nightmare. Why couldn't she see that allowing a stray dog in my home wasn't a good idea?

"You'll clean that up, too. It's not the end of the world if that happens."

"What about your house?" I persisted. "He could stay with you."

She shook her head. "There's Sherlock to consider. Besides, the dog likes you, not me."

That seemed to be true. He was far more comfortable with me handling him than Aunt Tilde, although she made up for that by offering him plenty of treats. By the end, he reluctantly allowed her to pet him.

But giving him a bath and a brush was one thing. It was quite another to let him inside my apartment. It was only when I finally took a look inside the garage and saw the mess for myself that I relented.

"But only until Monday," I told Aunt Tilde as she helped me get him settled in.

"Of course," she said. We watched him flop down on his new bed after taking his time to sniff every nook and cranny of his new area.

That night, he had no issues sleeping in his bed. And the next morning, he promptly went potty when I took him outside, ate extra helpings of his food, accompanied me on a nice walk, and slept in the sun as I worked.

I had to admit, having him around was nicer than I'd thought. But that didn't mean I was planning on keeping him. I was in no position to have any sort of pet, much less a dog. I had no job, or at least no job that provided me a paycheck, no money, and no car. Eventually, I would have to do something to change all of that, and that would likely mean moving somewhere else. So, having a dog was most definitely out of the question.

Still, I couldn't help but feel my chest tighten as I said goodbye to him Monday morning. His brown eyes watched me sadly as I locked the door behind me.

"Where's the dog?" Aunt Tilde asked as I made my way to the car. She was in the middle of arranging Sherlock in the backseat.

"Still in the apartment. I figured when I was ready to bring him to the humane society, I'd come home and get him."

"Nonsense," she said, brushing her hands together as she stood up. "He can come with us."

I stared at the cat crate in the backseat. "But there's no room."

"There's plenty of room. Why come all the way back here? That's silly."

"Well … okay." I wasn't sure why I felt reluctant to bring him. Aunt Tilde was right; it would make it easier to just have him at work with me.

"And bring his bed," she called out as I started to walk back.

I turned around. "His bed? Why?"

Aunt Tilde gave me a look. "He's got to lie down somewhere while we work, right? Don't you want him to be comfortable?"

She had a point. Despite eating multiple helpings of dog food, he was still a bag of bones. Lying on the floor would be uncomfortable.

The moment I opened the door, he greeted me, wagging his tail and sniffling me like I had been gone a week. He bounded down the stairs and immediately settled into the backseat.

"See, this makes much more sense," Aunt Tilde said as I watched him and Sherlock nose each other, reminding me of the reason I had the dog in my apartment in the first place.

"You told me you didn't want the dog in your house because of Sherlock," I said.

"Did I?" Aunt Tilde asked, her voice innocent as she started the car.

I gave her a hard look. "Yes, you did. And now it's okay to bring both of them to the office? The office is much smaller than your house."

"Everyone's office is much smaller than their house," she said. "And Sherlock is used to sharing the office with other people and animals. Look at Smoke."

"I don't think Sherlock appreciates Smoke," I said.

She glanced at the rearview mirror. "Well, yeah. Smoke can be a little … aggressive. But he means well. I think."

I thought that was a little charitable, but didn't argue the point.

"Besides, look at those two! They're going to be great friends," she said.

My heart twisted inside me. *I have no business having a dog,* I reminded myself. "I'm taking him to the humane society today, you know."

Aunt Tilde hummed. "Of course. Do you have a name yet?"

"No, I don't have a name. Why would I name a dog I'm bringing to the humane society?" I asked.

"It might make it easier for the paperwork, if he has a name," she said.

I sat back in the seat, mulling over what she said. I actually had thought of a name. Scout. My favorite book as a child was *To Kill a Mockingbird*. And the name seemed to fit him. I had even called him Scout a couple of times, and he had immediately responded, like he knew it was his name.

"No," I said and stared out the window. Neither of us spoke the rest of the way to the agency.

Chapter 10

As the humane society didn't open until after ten, the dog bed ended up being a good choice. Both animals immediately settled right in—Sherlock on her cat tower and the dog on his pillow right next to it.

"It's like they've known each other forever," Aunt Tilde said.

They *were* hanging out like best friends. The pang in my chest was back, but I pushed it away and busied myself at my desk, reminding myself again that I had no business keeping a dog.

The bell at the door tinkled. "Good morning!" Nora called out cheerily. "I wanted to get an update on our new case before I open the bookstore … ack!"

Smoke had shot forward from between Nora's legs, nearly tripping her and causing her olive-green peasant skirt to billow up. He made a beeline to Sherlock, who was already standing up, her hackles raised on the back of her neck.

Woof!

Scout had leaped to his feet and was standing between the cat tower and Smoke. Smoke skittered to a halt in front of him. They stared at each other, the dog towering over Smoke, who was looking more and more unsure about the situation.

"Oh, look, Smoke. A new animal friend," Nora said happily as Smoke began to slink away. After a moment, Scout laid back down, but he still kept his eyes on Smoke, who was now on the other side of the room, his expression aloof, like he wanted everyone to know it was his idea he was over there. "What's his name?"

"He's a stray," I said. "We're taking him to the humane society later today."

Nora's face fell. "Oh, that's too bad. He's such a beautiful dog. Why don't you keep him?"

"It's better this way," I said, trying to focus on the checklist in front of me. I could practically feel Scout's sad brown eyes staring at the back of my head.

No, I wasn't going there.

"So, the case," Aunt Tilde said briskly. "It's going to be a big day. We're going to see Hal in jail. Do you want to come?"

My head shot up. "You are? When?" *And who's driving*, I wanted to ask, but didn't. Hal was being held in a Riverview jail, which was roughly an hour away.

Aunt Tilde glanced at her watch. "We should leave in an hour."

"An hour? What about the humane society?" I had been hoping to be there right at ten. The sooner the better. The longer I had him, the more attached he was going to get, and that wasn't fair to him.

"We can go in the afternoon when we're back. There's no rush," Aunt Tilde said.

I opened my mouth to argue when her words sunk in. "We? Who's going?"

"Well, all of us, of course," Aunt Tilde said. "We're all working the case."

"All of us?" I was starting to wonder if this was ever going to be a profitable business. "But … wouldn't it be better if we each took a piece of the case? Or maybe divide up the cases, so we're all not doing the same work?"

Aunt Tilde waved a hand. "We will, but I thought all of us hearing what Hal has to say is important. After that, we can figure out how to move forward."

It occurred to me that maybe Aunt Tilde wasn't sure what the next step would be, and was hoping the interview with Hal would make it clearer.

"I'd love to go with you, but I probably shouldn't leave the store," Nora said sadly. "I'm going to have to find some help if we're going to have more cases."

"You can keep an eye on the animals," Aunt Tilde said.

I looked over at Scout and Sherlock, who were both curled up on their respective beds, although Scout was still keeping an eye on everything. Nora had opened up one of the desk drawers and was poking through the contents and paying no attention to the animals. "Nora, are you sure you're okay with this?"

"Of course," Nora said, still not looking up. "Smoke loves other animals."

At that, I was even more convinced I should stay behind.

"They'll be fine," Aunt Tilde said. "They're best friends."

The sharp pang hit me in the chest again. "What if we get a walk-in, and Nora is in her bookstore? No one will be here to greet them?"

"We just leave a note on the door to go see Nora," Aunt Tilde said as Nora nodded.

I wasn't sure if I was ever going to get my head around how strangely this business was being run.

Before I could say anything else, Mildred came bustling in, complaining about the traffic. Aunt Tilde introduced her to Scout, who, for his part, got up from his bed to give her a welcoming sniff.

"Oh, hi, Emily! I was looking forward to having you over for dinner last night. Maybe next Saturday will be better for you?" Mildred asked brightly.

My stomach seemed to sink into the floor. "Maybe," I said quickly before changing the subject. "Aunt Tilde, since Mildred is here, should we get going?"

"Almost," Aunt Tilde said. "We just have to wait for one more person, who I think just pulled up." She craned her neck as she stared out the window.

I started tidying my desk, assuming she was talking about Greta. I heard the door open, and a male voice said, "Sorry I'm late."

I whirled around to see Nick standing there, looking a little more pulled together than he had last week, with his shirt buttoned up and his tie straight. He caught my eye and flashed me a crooked smile. I ignored him. "He's coming?"

"How else is he going to ask Hal questions?" Aunt Tilde asked, picking up her purse.

Scout had moseyed over to the door to sniff Nick, who ruffled his neck. "Who is this handsome fellow?"

"No one," I snapped as Scout leaned into his fingers. Traitor.

Nick glanced at me and raised an eyebrow. "No one?"

"Emily, why don't you drive with Nick, and Mildred can come

with me?" Aunt Tilde suggested, giving the dog a pat. "He's staying here to keep an eye on the place."

Nick's grin widened as I stared at Aunt Tilde in a panic. No, I absolutely couldn't be stuck in the car by myself with Nick for an hour. That was completely unacceptable. "Why can't I go with you?"

"Because Nick doesn't need to be driving all the way to Riverview by himself," Aunt Tilde said.

Mildred looked almost as alarmed as I felt. "Tilde, that's a terrible idea."

"You volunteering to drive with Nick?" Aunt Tilde asked.

"What? No," Mildred said, looking almost as horrified as Nick did at that suggestion.

"So, it's settled. Emily will go with Nick," Aunt Tilde said.

"Why are we taking so many cars?" I asked. "There's only four of us. We can all fit in one, right?"

"I have to do some errands after we see Hal," Aunt Tilde said.

Those mysterious errands again. "We could all go with you," I said.

Aunt Tilde shook her head. "Absolutely not. Both you and Nick have better things to do than come along on my errands."

"And I don't?" Mildred asked.

"Would you rather drive yourself?" Aunt Tilde asked.

Mildred glared at her. "Fine." She turned to Nick and shook her finger at him. "Behave yourself. Remember, she's taken."

Nick held out his hands, palms out. "I promise I will be on my best behavior."

Mildred didn't look convinced, but at least she didn't argue. Instead, she followed Aunt Tilde out to the parking lot with a huff.

Nick finished petting the dog and stood up. Scout bumped his nose into his leg. "We should probably get going before they get too much of a head start."

I didn't move. No, this was not happening. I had plenty of work to do. I should just stay here.

But before I could make my excuses, Nora chimed in. "Don't worry, Emily. I've got this under control."

"See, everything is taken care of," Nick said, pushing the door open. "Besides, don't you want to hear what Hal has to say for yourself?"

Ugh. I wanted to scratch that smirk off of his face again. Especially since he was right.

Double ugh. What a way to start off the week.

***

"What brings you to Redemption?" Nick asked as we sped down the highway in his cherry-red Mustang convertible. The car was cleaner than I expected, although I did spy some crumpled fast-food bags and file folders in the back.

"My aunt lives here," I said, even though it didn't exactly answer the question.

He rolled his eyes. "I know that. Why did you decide to move here and start working at the Redemption Detective Agency?"

"I needed a change," I said, turning my head to look out the window. A herd of black-and-white cows were grazing on a large patch of grass.

"This is surely quite a change," he agreed. "Especially compared to Riverview. That's where you were living, right?"

I turned to give him a sideways glance. He was looking straight ahead, his strong, capable hands relaxed on the steering wheel and his expression open, like he was making small talk at a cocktail party. But behind that friendly exterior, I could almost feel the predator prowling about, testing the edges, looking for weakness.

"Why the twenty questions?" I asked.

He shrugged. "Why not? We have a long drive ahead of us, and I'd like to get to know Tilde's niece."

"There's really nothing to tell," I assured him. "I'm pretty boring."

"Oh, I doubt that." There was laughter in his voice. "You seem the exact opposite of boring."

Hot shame flooded my cheeks as an unwelcome memory popped into my head. *Look, it's nothing personal. We're just not a good match. I just need someone a little more … well, exciting. You've been great; don't get me wrong. We've had some good times. But you must feel it too … how things have gotten a little stale?*

Sure, the initial rush of passion had faded, but wasn't that supposed to happen when you're building a life together? The honeymoon phase wasn't supposed to last forever.

I gave my head a quick shake. Now was not the time to dissect my relationship with Geoff. Actually, it would never be the time. He was a part of my past, and I needed to focus on the future.

"Earth to Emily."

I blinked to see Nick watching me out of the corner of his eye. "Sorry. What did you say?"

"I was saying it must be one heck of a story that got you to Redemption," he said.

"Why are you being so persistent?" I asked.

"The same thing that makes me such a good lawyer. I have a hunch there's a lot more hiding behind that pretty face." He eyed me as he flashed a quick smile. "Plus, I'm intrigued."

I pushed down the irrational warmth at his calling me pretty, telling myself that just because he said it, didn't mean he meant it. For heaven's sake, he was a lawyer and most likely a charmer. I should be skeptical of everything he said. "About what?"

"You."

My stomach flipped, and I let out an awkward laugh in an attempt to cover it up. "Me? There's nothing intriguing about me."

"Oh, I think there is." He glanced in his driver's side mirror before smoothly changing lanes. "You're way too smart to be living above Tilde's garage and working on her latest hobby. I mean, Tilde's great. I owe my life to her. But something dramatic would have had to happen for you to end up here."

My cheeks were hot, and I turned away, lest he think I was blushing because I wasn't used to compliments—even the throwaway type like he had just given me. Never mind that I *wasn't* used to compliments. I tried to turn the focus away from me. "Why do you owe your life to Aunt Tilde?"

I expected some sort of snappy remark, but instead, he was quiet for so long, I twisted in my seat to look at him. He met my eyes and gave me a quick smile, but there was something forced about it.

"I didn't have a great childhood," he said. "Mother was a

drunk, father was never home. Either working or with one of his mistresses." His voice held a touch of bitterness. "I didn't deal with it very well. I had a bit of a wild streak in me, and by the time I was in high school, I was definitely on a path that was leading to either jail or death. Fighting, drinking, skipping school, stealing cars, you name it. One night, I picked a fight I had no business picking, and it didn't go well. Luckily, someone called the cops, or it might have ended very badly. The cops took me to the hospital, which is where I met Tilde. She was my nurse."

His fingers tightened on the steering wheel. "I'm not sure what she saw in me. I was very angry, very distrustful, especially of adults. But somehow, she saw through that. The cops had tried to call my parents, but no one picked up, probably because my mother was passed out and my father wasn't home. Tilde knew the cops who had brought me in and was able to talk them into letting her take care of me. She actually took me to her house and let me spend the night. In the morning, she made me breakfast, replaced my bandages, and drove me to my parents. Neither one of them ever knew I hadn't been home that night, nor did either of them ask what happened to me." He grimaced at the memory, running his hands roughly through his hair.

"Anyway," he continued after a moment, "Tilde made a point of checking in with me. She gave me her number before she dropped me off at home and insisted I either come by the hospital or her house every day so she could make sure I was healing properly. I thought it was silly, but I did it. And then I kept coming over, even when everything was healed. She would feed me, listen to me, nag me to go to class and do my homework." He chuckled a little at the memory. "She was the one who encouraged me to go to college, and once I was on board, she helped me not only apply to schools, but for scholarships and financial aid packages. I owe her a lot."

I fidgeted in my seat. Nick's story hit uncomfortably close to home. I wasn't sure how I felt about it. "Aunt Tilde is good at that … being there for you when others aren't."

He glanced at me, and a shared understanding passed between us. "Yeah, she is."

I looked away, feeling even more awkward. "I didn't realize

she was doing that. Helping you, I mean. She never mentioned anything."

He gave me a knowing glance. "I wouldn't imagine she would. Just like she never said anything to me about anyone else."

Oof. Point taken.

"So, what about you?" he asked, a teasing note in his voice. "Now that I've told you about my tragic upbringing, how about sharing yours?"

"That's why you did it? To guilt me into telling you my story?" I asked, my voice light even as my mind whirled around, searching for a way out of it.

He raised an eyebrow. "Did it work?"

I clenched my fists. *Unfortunately, yes.* "It's really nothing special. Just another sad story about losing a job, an apartment, a car, and a fiancé. Believe me when I say it's not worth talking about."

I braced myself, waiting for the inevitable sympathetic words, most of them empty or fake. Or a barrage of questions.

But he did neither. Instead, he went in a completely unexpected direction. "Are you aware of Redemption's history?"

I shot him a funny look. "What?"

He flashed me a quick grin. "I know, it sounds a little random, but stay with me for a moment."

"If you're talking about how Redemption was founded by the children whose parents disappeared, yes, I'm familiar with that."

"Are you also aware that a lot of us who live here think Redemption decides who lives here?"

I vaguely remembered hearing something like that over the years. "That's silly. A town isn't a person. It can't make decisions like that."

Nick shrugged. "True. Except it doesn't explain why some people can't move here, or leave, even if they want to."

"That happens everywhere," I said. "People can't always do what they want to do."

"It also doesn't explain the very strange circumstances that either lead them here or send them on their way," Nick persisted.

I rolled my eyes. "I know Redemption has a reputation for a lot of unexplained and odd things going on, but that doesn't mean the town is sentient. And it certainly doesn't mean it has any influence over people's lives."

Nick inclined his head. "Fair enough. But if it was possible that Redemption is able to 'influence' people and attract the ones it wants here and repel the ones it doesn't, perhaps that's the real reason why you're here."

I stared at him. "Wait. You're saying you think my life imploded because Redemption wanted me to move here?"

He flipped on his turn signal to change lanes. "Why not? It got you here, right?"

For a moment, I couldn't even formulate an answer. The idea was preposterous. My life unraveled because I started digging into something that, in retrospect, I should have left alone.

Now that he put the idea in my head, though, I couldn't help but start turning it over and examining it from different angles. It WAS a little ... disconcerting, how quickly everything fell apart. My job, my fiancé. And once those were gone, the rest quickly followed. I drove a company car, so when I lost my job, I lost my car.

But that was probably more of an indication of how naïve I had been, rather than having anything to do with Redemption.

Still ...

"Even if that were the case, that Redemption was somehow behind it," I finally said—Nick smirked, but I ignored him—"why me? I wasn't looking to leave Riverview. So why?"

"Why does anything happen?" Nick asked. "If you are supposed to be here, and you didn't realize it, it sounds to me like you needed a huge upheaval in your life to get you to move."

Even though I knew intellectually that was ridiculous, there was something to it that felt uncomfortably close to the truth.

"It looks like we're here," Nick said, slowing down and putting on his blinker to turn into the parking lot. I could see the prison beyond the seemingly endless miles of gates and barbed wire—a stark-gray building that looked depressing even with the sun shining on it. Just looking at it from the outside gave me the shivers. I couldn't imagine how I would feel having to live in it.

Especially if I were innocent.

Nick pulled into an empty parking space, and we both got out in time to watch Aunt Tilde drive up in the pink Cadillac. There was a cool breeze, which was nice, but even the fresh air couldn't cover up the underlying stink of hopelessness and despair.

"Oh, Emily," Nick said casually.

I had been watching Aunt Tilde park a little too close to a blue Ford pickup truck while trying not to wince, but I glanced over at him.

He was leaning against the back of the car, and with the wind mussing his dark hair, he looked like a model. I could feel my heart flip and told myself to stop it.

"Yes?"

His green eyes were serious as they met mine. "If you're ever ready to tell me the real story of what happened to you, I'm a good listener. I even might be able to help."

I looked away. Aunt Tilde was backing up, presumably to give Mildred a little bit of room to get out, but all she managed to do was get even closer to that truck. "No one can help. It was all just … I should have known better."

He cocked his head. "Maybe. Maybe not. Just know, when you're ready, I'm here." He flashed me that cocky grin of his. "And I'm very good at keeping secrets."

I could feel a blush start to warm my cheeks, but before I could respond, Aunt Tilde was calling us over. "Hey! Come on you two. We don't want to be late."

Chapter 11

"Who are you?"

Hal stared at us, his expression confused. We were crammed into a small conference room that had a cheap, chipped wooden table and two plain wooden chairs, one on each side. After Nick convinced the intake personnel that all four of us needed to be in there, a short, balding guard with a beer gut brought in three metal folding chairs.

Nick smiled and gestured at the wooden chair. "Come, sit."

Hal didn't move. He had light-brown hair, cut short, and large, brown, puppy-dog eyes framed with thick lashes that were wasted on a man. I suspected before he was incarcerated, he would have been considered good-looking. The orange jumpsuit certainly wasn't doing him any favors, nor the sallowness of his skin due to rarely being outside. There were dark purple circles under his eyes, too. "I was told my lawyer was here." His voice was suspicious.

Nick's smiled widened. "That's one of the things I want to talk to you about. Come sit."

Hal rolled his eyes. "My mother sent you, didn't she?" His voice was heavy. "Look. I'll tell you what I told the other guy. I confessed. I pled guilty. There's nothing more to be done."

Nick's gaze sharpened. "Really?" He picked up his pen and jotted a note on his yellow pad.

"So hiring the attorney wasn't your idea?" Aunt Tilde asked.

He sighed and ran his hand through his hair. "No, of course not. I told her he was just a con artist, promising her something he couldn't deliver. But she wouldn't listen." His gaze softened, and I could see the deep sadness in his eyes. He blinked and gave himself a quick shake. "Anyway, if you're here to scam my mother as well, I feel like I should tell you she is out of money, so you're out of luck. Now, if you'll excuse me ..." He started to turn toward the door where the guards waited outside.

Nick shoved his metal chair back with a loud grating noise and stood up as well. "I think we got off on the wrong foot. My name is Nick Stewart, and I am an attorney. If we do come to an arrangement and I represent you, it would be pro bono."

Hal gave him a suspicious look. "Why would you do that?"

Nick shot him a level look. "Because I don't like seeing desperate people like your mother being taken advantage of by unscrupulous lawyers."

Hal considered that for a moment, then took a second look at the three of us. His face blanched as he finally recognized Mildred. "Ms. Schmidt? What are you doing here?"

"We're part of the Redemption Detective Agency," Mildred said.

He looked at her in confusion. "Detective agency?"

"Yes, your mom wanted us to look into your case," Aunt Tilde said. "We're not charging her either."

He looked harder at Aunt Tilde. "I know you, too."

"Tilde Tillerson," Aunt Tilde said. "And this is my niece, Emily."

I gave him a little wave. He didn't look impressed.

"So, I'm okay talking to you," he pointed at Nick. "Especially if you can help my mother understand this is the way things have to be, and she needs to stop wasting money on charlatans. But you three …" he waved at us. "While I'm glad you're not charging her, there's nothing to look into. It's done. I'm guilty. That's it."

Aunt Tilde folded her hands on top of the table. "It might help your mother move on if she understood why you confessed."

"I confessed because I'm guilty," he snapped.

"That's nonsense," Mildred said, rapping her knuckles on the table. "You're no killer. Now stop this silliness right now and tell us why you would confess to a crime you didn't commit."

Hal looked taken aback. "Um … Ms. Schmidt, I …"

Mildred straightened up, folding her arms across her chest and leveling a look at him that made me feel like I had just been caught passing notes in class. I was suddenly grateful I had never had her as a teacher. "Now, Hal. I mean it. This nonsense has gone on long enough. Our prisons are overcrowded as it is. We don't need innocent people making the situation worse."

Hal looked visibly torn. I had to hand it to Mildred. Who would have thought you could turn a fake confession into a guilt trip?

Aunt Tilde put a hand on Mildred's arm. "Let's start with you walking us through your confession. If we all understand why you killed your best friend, and I include your mother in this, it might be easier for her to move on."

A muscle in Hal's cheek twitched. "He wasn't my friend. At least, not anymore."

Aunt Tilde cocked her head. "Is that the reason why you killed him? Because you weren't friends anymore?"

He worked his jaw. "It wasn't like that. I didn't mean to kill him. It was an accident."

Mildred rolled her eyes and muttered something that sounded like "An accident, my foot."

"So what happened?" Aunt Tilde asked.

He folded his arms across his chest and looked away. "We were at a party. We were both drinking. I know I was drinking too much. We argued. I pushed him. He fell and hit his head. End of story."

"What did you argue about?"

His throat worked as he swallowed. "It doesn't matter. He's still dead, right?"

"True, but it would be good to know."

He shrugged. "We argued. We were doing that a lot back then. I had too much to drink and overreacted. Like I said, end of story."

Aunt Tilde and Mildred glanced at each other. "Why weren't you friends anymore?" Aunt Tilde asked.

He shook his head. "We just drifted apart. That happens, especially senior year. After graduation, we were going in separate directions."

Aunt Tilde chewed on her bottom lip. "Hal." Her voice was gentle. "If you want people, like your mother, like your former teacher, to believe your confession, explaining what was going on between you two would go a long way in helping everyone move on."

"I don't know why everyone keeps trying to make a big deal out of this," he said, throwing his hands up. "Look, it's over. I made a mistake. A big one, and I'm paying for it. Please, just leave it alone. Okay?"

"Hal, wait," Nick said as Hal strode toward the door and started banging for the guard.

"No, we're done here," Hal said. "I don't want to talk about this anymore. I've made my peace with it, and everyone else needs to, as well."

"But what about your mother and that other lawyer?" Nick asked as the guard appeared at the door.

Hal looked at him. "If you can help her get her money back, I'll help you. But that's it. No more about me or my confession. Got it?"

Before any of us could answer, the same guard that brought him in led him away from the room.

***

"That went well," I said sarcastically as we stood together in the parking lot next to the pink Cadillac.

"Such a stubborn boy," Mildred said. "He wasn't always so stubborn. I don't know what got into him."

"Prison might do that to you," Nick said drily.

Mildred let out a huff. "Still. That wasn't the sweet boy who was in my classroom. I can see why his mom is so upset with him. He definitely needs our help. What's the plan?"

Nick rubbed the back of his neck. "far be it from me to argue," he said carefully. "But Hal did seem pretty clear about not wanting our help."

"Fiddlesticks," Mildred said. "That boy needs our help, and that's what we're going to do. Right, Tilde?"

Tilde drummed her fingers on the car's trunk. "Emily, what do you think?"

I was taken aback. "Me? Why are you asking me?"

"Why not?" A faint smile touched her lips. "As our new office manager, you should weigh in on this conversation. Do you think we should drop it like Nick says? Tell Greta that her son doesn't want to be helped, and he did plead guilty? Or should we do what Mildred suggests and pursue it despite Hal's objections?"

I paused, considering. Until that moment, I had assumed we were going to continue investigating despite what Hal had said, and even if I wanted to stop it, I wouldn't be able to.

But Aunt Tilde's question threw me. What *did* I think we should do? I kept picturing how ill at ease Hal was, standing there in his orange jumpsuit. Of course, in his defense, we had tricked him, so was it that surprising he didn't want to trust us?

Although he did know Aunt Tilde and Mildred, so it wasn't like we were complete strangers.

Still, we hadn't been honest. I couldn't blame him for not wanting anything to do with us.

That said, there was something deeper going on. The way he kept ducking his head and refusing to make eye contact, the nervous way he shifted his weight from foot to foot.

He was lying about something. The question was, what?

"While I can see Nick's point about doing what Hal wants us to do," I said slowly. "And, since Hal made it clear he's open to working with Nick, Nick may not want to be a part of this. But Hal is NOT our client. Greta is. And despite Hal's wish that Greta simply get over his confession, I don't think she's going to. At least not without a clear motive. This 'We got into a fight, but I'm not going to tell anyone what the fight was about' isn't going to cut it. You don't accidentally kill someone because you're drifting apart, I don't care how drunk you are. I think, for Greta's sake, we owe it to her to give her some closure. Because we all know she's not going to stop until she's either cleared her son's name or understands why he killed Rocco."

Aunt Tilde was nodding as I spoke. "Agreed. We keep going. And with that …" She popped open the trunk and started fishing around. "Crap. Those library books are still here. Emily, you have to remind me to return these books."

I struggled to not roll my eyes. "Of course."

She emerged from the trunk, file folder in hand, and slammed it shut. "Okay, so I got a list from Greta of all the attendees of the party. Most of the people didn't know either Rocco or Hal, but there were about a half dozen who did." She dug a couple of typed sheets of paper out of the folder and laid them on the trunk. "These here with the asterisk," she tapped near the top, "knew them best. The rest of them were more like passing acquaintances."

I craned my neck to look at the list. The name "Fern" jumped out at me. "Is Fern Hal's girlfriend?"

"No, Rocco's girlfriend," Aunt Tilde said.

Something dinged in the back of my head. "I'll talk to her," I said.

Aunt Tilde nodded and produced a pen to make a note on the sheet.

"George Gibson," Nick said. "I know him. I'll talk to George."

I gave him a surprised look. "I didn't think you were going to help."

Nick shrugged. "I realized you're right. Greta is my client."

Aunt Tilde made a note. "Great. Mildred, you and I can divide up the other three. Em, we'll have to figure out a schedule with the car, so let me know ..."

"I can drive her," Nick said smoothly.

I gaped at him. "What?"

"In fact, Emily and I can interview both George and Fern," Nick continued, as if I hadn't said anything.

"Perfect," Aunt Tilde said as Nick scribbled down the contact information for both Fern and George on his legal pad.

"I don't like this," Mildred said darkly as she glared at Nick.

"I don't either," I said. "Don't I get a say?"

"Of course you get a say," Aunt Tilde said. "But don't you think it will be far easier to just have Nick drive you than to try and coordinate with me?"

Ugh. I gritted my teeth. She had a point.

Aunt Tilde seemed to read my mind, because she patted my shoulder. "It won't be long before we get the car sorted out. Having Nick drive you around is just temporary."

"It better be," Mildred muttered.

I couldn't agree more.

Chapter 12

We found Fern at work. Employed by the town of Redemption, she came out to greet us as we waited in the lobby of the town building.

"Can I help you?" she asked, looking at us curiously. She was very petite, with long brunette hair and dark-brown eyes.

Nick flashed her one of his charming signature grins. "I'm Nick Stewart, and this is Emily. I'm an attorney, and your name came up in reference to one of my clients. I'm hoping you have a few minutes to chat with us."

She stared at us. "Attorney?" Her voice was faint as she lifted a hand to the collar of her white silk shirt that she had paired with a slim black skirt. Behind her, the sharp-faced woman who sat behind the receptionist's desk leaned forward. "Who is the client?"

Nick's smile didn't falter. "I'd rather not say. Could we talk in private? I promise it won't take long." He made a small gesture with his head toward the nosy receptionist.

The blood seemed to leach from Fern's face as understanding dawned, and she swallowed hard before nodding and leading us down the hall to an empty conference room.

"What's going on?" she asked the moment the door was closed behind us. "Is someone in trouble?"

"In a manner of speaking," Nick said. His body was relaxed, as if he were trying to put her at ease, but I could see a sharpness in his green eyes as he studied her. "It's about Hal Jarrett."

She blanched. "Hal? What about him? Did something happen to him in prison?" Her expression was alarmed, and she took a step toward Nick.

Nick quickly shook his head. "Hal is fine. I just saw him today."

She closed her eyes briefly, sucking in a quick breath before re-focusing on Nick, this time with a more skeptical look. "So, I don't understand. Why are you here? That case is over. Hal confessed."

"Maybe we should sit down," Nick suggested, gesturing toward the chairs around the conference table.

Fern folded her arms across her chest. "Not until I understand why you're here."

Nick shrugged and leaned against the table as he flashed her another smile. "We're looking into the legalities of Hal's confession, which means re-interviewing some of the witnesses ... like yourself."

Fern went very still. "Hal's confession may not have been legal? What does that mean? Could he get out of prison?"

"That's one possibility," Nick said, gesturing again to the chairs. "We just have a few questions to ask, and then we'll be on our way. Can we sit?"

Fern chewed on the bottom of her lower lip before nodding slightly and taking a chair. Nick and I settled ourselves on the other side. I (begrudgingly) had to hand it to Nick—his lawyer-speak was so convincing, even I was starting to believe we had a shot at getting Hal out of prison.

Nick pulled out his yellow notepad and pen. "You were Rocco's girlfriend, right?"

She nodded, clasping her hands in front of her. She seemed so small and frail sitting in that chair, and I could feel my heart go out to her.

"I'm sorry for your loss," Nick said gravely.

"I am too," I said.

Fern inclined her head. "Thank you."

He hesitated a moment. "If it isn't too painful, can you tell me a little about your relationship?"

She squeezed her hands tighter. "What do you want to know?"

"Just the basics," Nick said. "Like, how long did you date, and when did you meet? That sort of thing."

She sucked in a deep breath. "We met freshman year. Felix, that's my twin brother, lived on the same dorm floor as Rocco and Hal. They immediately clicked and started hanging out together, so it was only a matter of time before I met them." She smiled faintly. "It was at a party, and the moment I looked at him, I was sure he was 'the one.' We were together from that day on until … well …" Her voice trailed off.

Nick cleared his throat. "Again, my condolences. Your relationship was still good then? No problems?"

She lifted a shoulder delicately. "Every couple has problems, but yes, things were good. We were talking about getting married and starting a family after graduation."

Nick's eyebrows rose. "Oh? I didn't realize you were engaged."

She shifted in her seat. "Officially, we weren't. Rocco wanted to wait until after we graduated and were settled into our careers. Then, we'd get married."

Nick nodded as he jotted down a note. "What about Hal? Did you meet him at that same party?"

She shook her head. "No, he wasn't there that night. I met him a few weeks later, after Rocco and I were dating."

"What was your relationship like? Were you friends, or …"

"Yes, we were friends," Fern said. "Hal was always very sweet to me." She stared at her clenched hands. "I still can't believe it."

"You still can't believe Hal killed Rocco?"

She nodded tersely but didn't look at us.

"How was Hal and Rocco's relationship?"

"They were friends. Best friends." She finally looked up at us, and I could see her eyes were damp. "I know it was an accident, but still."

"Do you know what they were fighting about that night?"

Fern shook her head. "No. Not really. I know they had a few disagreements that last year, mostly over money. Something about a rent check that wasn't paid or something … I don't know."

Nick frowned. "So the fight that night was about money?"

Fern's eyes widened. "What? No, I'm sure … I was just saying, I know they had a few … disagreements going on, including one about money … but I don't know what they were fighting about that night."

It couldn't be more obvious that she was lying; she might as well as had "liar" tattooed across her forehead. But Nick didn't challenge her. "What about the party itself? Did you notice anything off?"

"No, not really," Fern said.

Nick gave her a curious look. "But you were his girlfriend. You must have seen something. Didn't you hang out together?"

She straightened up. "Of course we hung out together. But just because we were dating doesn't mean we were attached at the hip." Her voice had turned to ice. "We still had our own friends."

Nick held out a hand. "My mistake. I didn't mean to offend. I'm just trying to get a sense of what happened that night. So, you were with other friends?"

Her expression softened slightly. "Mostly. I was with my friend Gemini, and Rocco was with his friends. At least, that's what I assumed." Her voice hardened ever so slightly.

"So, when you found out Rocco was dead …" Nick began.

"Was when everyone else found out," she finished. "Hal ran out into the living room shouting for a phone, saying Rocco had fallen in one of the bedrooms and needed an ambulance. All hell broke loose, as you can imagine. It was only later that Hal changed his story, claiming he had killed Rocco." She glanced at the clock, then stood up and smoothed out her skirt, her demeanor businesslike. "I'm going to have to cut this short. I didn't realize how late it is. I have to get back to work."

Nick stood up as well. "Here's my card, in case you can think of anything else that might be helpful."

She took it, her mouth puckered in distaste, and I had a feeling she was going to toss it in the garbage the moment she got back to her office. "I hope you'll be able to help Hal. He doesn't … he doesn't deserve this punishment."

"He killed someone," Nick said gravely. "By his own admission. You don't think he should be punished?"

"I didn't say that," she said. "But he said it was an accident, and I'm sure it was. It doesn't matter how long Hal sits in prison; it's not going to bring Rocco back, and I don't think Hal's life should be destroyed, too."

Nick cocked his head. "I'm surprised to hear you say that. Rocco was your boyfriend."

"And Hal was my friend," she said, and I could see the sheen of tears back in her eyes. "That night, I lost both of them. Is it so

96

wrong to wish I could have one of them back?"

"Of course not," I said, stepping forward to grasp her hand. It was ice cold, and I squeezed it gently. "It was a terrible tragedy for everyone."

Fern looked a little startled, but then a tiny smile touched her lips. "Thank you. And now, forgive me, but I must get back to work."

She led us out of the conference room and back to the lobby. I waited until we had left the building before speaking. "She's lying."

Nick grinned at me. "Of course she is. Now, it's time for the fun part."

"What's the fun part?"

"Trying to figure out what she was lying about."

***

The dog greeted me the moment Nick and I walked into the agency, wagging his tail and rubbing against me. I stroked his neck and glanced at the clock. I really should take him to the humane society before it got much later, but I really didn't want to.

"He was a very good boy," Aunt Tilde, sitting at one of the desks, said. Mildred was at the other one, talking on the phone.

"He is a good boy," I agreed, watching him greet Nick before heading back to curl up in his bed.

Aunt Tilde watched me. "You know, you could keep him. I certainly don't mind if he's in your apartment."

"No," I said, slumping down in my chair. "I'm in no position to keep a dog. I'm not going to be living with you forever, and then what am I going to do?"

Aunt Tilde shrugged. "Take him with you?"

"I can't do that to him," I said. "What if my next apartment doesn't take dogs?"

"Then you find one that does," Nick said, leaning against the last empty desk.

I glared at him. "It's not that easy."

Nick flashed me a lazy grin that never failed to irritate me. "It can be."

Before I could think of a suitable retort, Aunt Tilde asked for an update on our conversation with Fern. While Nick filled her in, I started digging through the notes on my desk. Nora had taken a few messages for me in her loping handwriting that always took me a few moments to decipher. One was from the commercial cleaners I had hired to do a deep clean on the entire office, especially focusing on the kitchen. I wanted to book them for tomorrow, as tonight, the pest exterminator was coming, but I couldn't figure out whether the note was confirming an appointment for the next day or scheduling for Thursday. Nor could I be sure what time they were coming. I was thinking about walking over to the bookstore to ask Nora when the bell rang.

I turned to see a sleek black cat stroll into the agency. It was quite large with dark-green eyes. I looked around to see if there was a human behind it, but the cat appeared to be alone.

"Oh, Midnight," Aunt Tilde said. "Nice of you to stop by."

Midnight flicked his tail once, then headed over to the corner where Sherlock and Scout were hanging out and proceeded to greet them both.

"Midnight?" I asked.

"Charlie Kingsley's cat," Aunt Tilde said.

Midnight let out a loud meow.

"Or, I guess I should say, the cat that lives with Charlie," Aunt Tilde corrected herself as Nick chucked. "Sorry, Midnight."

I glanced back at the door. "Is Charlie here as well?"

Aunt Tilde peered in that direction as well. "Doesn't look like it. But that's not surprising. Midnight likes to make the rounds by himself."

I looked at her in surprise. "But where does Charlie live?"

"Oh …" Aunt Tilde waved her hand. "About ten minutes away or so. Maybe fifteen. Not too far."

"And the cat came here all by himself?"

"Midnight has a mind of his own," Nick said. "He does what he wants. You'll see."

"But how did he get in?" I looked at Nick. "Did you open the door?"

Nick held his hands up. "I didn't touch anything."

"Midnight is pretty resourceful," Aunt Tilde said.

"But opening a door?" I couldn't believe how blase they were being. A cat was wandering around miles from his home and could somehow open doors?

"One of my friends had a cat that could open doors," Mildred said. I wasn't sure when she had hung up the phone. "That cat could open any door in the house. It was a real pain, let me tell you. She ended up installing deadbolts to keep it from letting the dog and her toddler outside. It was a mess." She started thumbing through the stack of paper on her desk. "I'm glad you changed your mind about the dog. He's very sweet. What's his name?"

Scout lifted his head up from the bed and grinned.

I eyed her. "What are you talking about? What did I change my mind about?"

She gestured toward the dog. "Keeping him, of course." When I didn't immediately respond, she glanced up, her eyebrows knit in confusion. "You ARE keeping him, right? He's still here, after all, and the humane society closes soon …"

A sharp pain blossomed across my calf. "Ouch!" I looked down to see Midnight sitting in front of me with one paw up, his tail lashing. "You scratched me!"

There were five distinct scratch marks down my calf. Luckily, they weren't deep, but they still stung. "Why did you do that?"

Midnight stared at me, his green eyes unblinking.

Aunt Tilde was the one who answered. "I suspect he wants you to keep the dog."

I stared at Aunt Tilde. "What? That's silly. Hey!" Midnight swiped at my leg again, but this time, I was able to move away fast enough. "Stop that."

"Midnight has a soft spot for stray animals in Redemption," Aunt Tilde said. "When I adopted Sherlock, he made a point of visiting me, as well, to let me know he approved."

I glared at Midnight as I tucked my legs more tightly under me. "How can a cat know any of that? It's a cat."

"I wouldn't mess around with Midnight," Mildred said. "He has a reputation in Redemption. He's been around for years and years."

"This is ridiculous," I said as Midnight yawned and licked his whiskers, displaying a frightening array of very sharp teeth. "Cats don't understand English."

"Just like they don't open doors," Nick suggested, grinning at me. I scowled at him, which just widened his smile.

"You aren't helping," I hissed.

"Test it, if you don't believe us," Aunt Tilde said. "Say you're going to take the dog to the humane society and see what Midnight does."

I glowered at Midnight, whose tail was flicking dangerously. "Tomorrow, I'm going to drop Scout off at the huma-" I didn't even finish the sentence before Midnight started swatting at me again. "Ouch! Alright, alright. I'll give it a week. Okay?"

Midnight sat there, paw raised in the air, considering.

"I'm really not in any position to keep a dog," I said to the cat, feeling somewhat foolish talking to him directly ... even if he did look like he was listening to me. "But I'll give it a week, and then I'll reevaluate. Fair?"

Midnight blinked his eyes at me before turning around and trotting back to nuzzle Scout, who thumped his tail happily on the bed.

"Like we said, Midnight has a reputation," Mildred said.

I frowned at all three of them as I leaned down to rub where Midnight had scratched me. "Coincidence."

"Hmm," Mildred hummed as she turned her attention back to the paperwork.

"Scout is a nice name," Aunt Tilde said.

Chapter 13

I settled down at my desk with a fresh cup of coffee, listening to the sounds of the cleaning crew in the kitchen area. Scout and Sherlock were relaxed in their respective beds, and Aunt Tilde was off running errands.

Man, I really needed a car. Hopefully, Geoff would be getting back to me this week, like he'd promised. For the time being, I was attempting to draw up some plans for cheap ways to fix up the kitchen area, so we could start using it as office space.

The bell made its little tinkling sound, and I turned to see Nick walking in. "What are you doing here?"

"Good morning to you, too." He was carrying a white bag and a cardboard tray with two coffees. "I brought breakfast."

I gave him a suspicious look. "Why?"

"You wound me," he said dramatically, placing the bag and tray down on one of the desks so he could pet Scout, who had meandered over to greet him, tail wagging. Today, his button-down shirt was light pink, and he had paired it with a gray tie and pants. My heart gave a funny little skip at how good he looked. "Why wouldn't I bring you breakfast?"

"Because it makes no sense," I said. "We've just met."

He shrugged and opened up the white bag to pull out two muffins. "Blueberry or banana nut? Both are from Aunt May's Diner, along with the coffee."

"Whatever." I wanted to tell him I didn't want a muffin, but my stomach had started growling at the mention of them. I'd skipped breakfast earlier, not wanting to hold up Aunt Tilde from her errands. Man, I needed my own car.

"Well, if that's the case, I would recommend the blueberry. As much as I do love a good banana nut, Aunt May's is famous for their blueberry muffins," he said as he placed the muffin and coffee on my desk.

I stared at them. I wasn't sure what to do.

"You're welcome," Nick said, moving back to the desk where his coffee and muffin waited.

A hot flush of shame colored my cheeks. "Thank you. Sorry. I'm not used to people bringing me anything."

He cocked his head. "Really? Not even your fiancé?"

I ducked my head and started removing the paper from the muffin. "He did other things for me." Which didn't answer the question. Nor could I actually remember, in that moment, what those other things were. Other than taking his own sweet time to send me my money.

"Anyway," I continued, wanting to change the subject, "as much as I do appreciate you stopping by and bringing me breakfast, I still would like to know why. You must have lawyer work to do, right?"

He took a sip of coffee. "I do. I wanted to let you know I was able to get in touch with George, and we have a meeting set up for this afternoon at two. Will that work for you?"

"Yes, that's fine." I took a bite of the blueberry muffin and almost swooned. Nick was right—it was amazing.

"Great." He glanced at the kitchen, where the cleaning crew was making a lot of loud banging noises. "I was also curious about what you're going to do with this place."

I shrugged and looked down at my pathetic sketches. "I'm not sure. Why?"

"Because I might be able to help."

I stared at him. "You?"

"You're really doing a number on my ego today," he said drily.

My cheeks heated again. "But you're a lawyer."

"I am. But that doesn't mean I'm not handy with a hammer." He grinned at me as he took a bite of his muffin. "I could help with your renovations."

"You want to help?" I looked around the room, searching for a hidden camera. "Why?"

"I told you, because I owe Tilde a lot."

"Yes, but you're already helping with free legal services. You certainly don't need to be doing more free labor."

He inclined his head, as if conceding the point. "True, but if this is what Tilde wants—to turn this detective agency into a success—then I want to do what I can to help. And her spending money on a contractor when I don't mind doing the work seems like a waste to me." His dark-green eyes met mine. "I suspect you know what I'm talking about."

I turned away and busied myself moving papers around my desk. Considering I had spent every weekend plus an hour or two after work every day gardening, I couldn't really argue.

Nick shifted in his seat, and I heard him mutter something under his breath.

I glanced up. "What?"

He made a face as he started pushing the piles of paper around, too. "I just spilled some coffee. Such a klutz. Hey …" He picked up a long envelope. "This has your name on it."

"It does?"

He nodded. "Yeah, it's from a law firm. Emerson, Anderson, and Gray. In Riverview."

I jumped up from my desk. "Oh. Aunt Tilde must have forgotten to give that to me." That was Geoff's law firm. Hopefully, it meant he had sent a check.

His eyes were concerned as he handed it to me. "Everything okay?"

"Yes, it's fine. It's from my ex," I explained, tearing open the envelope. "I was expecting it."

I pulled the paper out of the envelope and unfolded it. A check fluttered to the desk. I snatched it up to look at the amount.

And blinked.

And blinked again.

"No, this can't be right," I said, prying the envelope open more to see if there was another check I had missed. There wasn't.

"What's going on?" Nick asked.

"I'm not sure," I said, grabbing the letter and nearly tearing it in my haste to unfold and read it. The more I read, the more I started to shake uncontrollably, my hands clutching the letter so tightly, it started to crumple. I felt like I had been slapped.

"Hey." Nick was suddenly right there, gently opening my

fingers to release the letter and placing it on the desk. "What happened?"

My jaw was clenched so tightly, I wasn't sure if I could answer without screaming, but I forced myself to loosen it and take a breath. "Geoff ... that's my ex. He ... well, it appears he *stole* almost twelve-thousand dollars from me."

Nick's eyes widened. "What?"

I closed my eyes. I felt so stupid. So incredibly stupid. How could I have gotten myself into this mess? I sucked in a deep breath, hating that I was going to have to confess how idiotic I had been but seeing no way around it. "When Geoff and I got engaged almost two years ago, I moved in with him." I kept my eyes closed, so I wouldn't have to see Nick's expression after he discovered how naïve I had been. "Geoff convinced me it would make sense to pool our money and have one checking account and one saving account. I was eager to get married and start a life together, so I wasn't keen about waiting to have the wedding. I agreed. Rather than opening up another account, Geoff told me he changed his account to a joint account and put my name on it. Like a fool, I believed him."

I squeezed my eyes shut tighter. "I didn't find out it *wasn't* a joint account until after he told me our relationship was over and I needed to move out. By then, it was too late. I had all my checks directly deposited into his account, including my severance package, which was over ten-thousand dollars, and my final paycheck."

"And you couldn't withdraw it?"

"I tried, but he had already removed me as a signer on the account."

Nick's eyes hardened. "He didn't immediately write you a check?"

I reached up to rub my forehead. "He said he needed to do a final accounting of my portion of the bills and would mail me a check for the remainder."

Nick's expression was exasperated. "How much time did he need? Couldn't he have done that while you were still in Riverview?"

My right eye started to twitch, and I reached up to rub my

forehead again. "He was in the middle of a big case. A lot of late nights and weekends. So, he said he needed to find the time to figure things out. He wanted to make sure it was accurate."

"Oh, I bet he wanted to make sure it was *accurate*," Nick said disgustedly. He nodded toward the check that had fallen upside down on the desk. "How much?"

I sucked in a breath. "Four-hundred thirty-two dollars and sixty-three cents."

His eyebrows went straight up. "Four hundred dollars? Out of ten thousand?"

"Over twelve thousand, when you include my final check," I said. Just saying it out loud made me want to scream in fury. How could he do this to me? My hands itched, wishing he was in front of me so I could slap him.

Nick reached for the check and flipped it over to see the amount for himself. "How did he come up with this amount? Or is this just the first check, and he'll be sending the rest at some point?"

"No, this is it. He claims …" My eye was twitching again. I shoved the letter toward Nick. "According to him, as he made more than me, we weren't actually splitting the household bills each month. He was paying more, so he figured out what my percentage should have been and then subtracted all of that from my severance and final paycheck."

Nick picked up the piece of paper and skimmed it. "I see he even gave you a mathematical example to explain it." He read from the letter. "'To simplify it, let's say your paycheck was a thousand dollars a month and mine was two thousand, and our expenses were three thousand. Obviously, those aren't the final numbers, but just to make it easier to follow, if you were to pay half—which would be fair—you would have needed to pay an additional five hundred dollars each month. While we were together, I didn't feel right saying anything, but now I feel like it's only fair to reconcile that difference.'" Nick let out a harsh laugh as he tossed the paper back onto my desk. "What a guy. At least he didn't charge you interest."

"Although he says he considered it," I said, my voice thick

with sarcasm as I rubbed my temples. "I guess I should be grateful he sent me something." It was all I could do to not snatch up the phone and let Geoff have it. Quite honestly, the only thing that was stopping me was that Nick was there, but the moment he was gone …

I couldn't believe he had done this to me. I truly, truly thought, at the end of the day, he would do the right thing. Sure, he dragged his feet a bit, and maybe he was a little too generous in terms of covering my portion of the bills when we were together, but I was expecting to lose maybe a few hundred.

Not over twelve thousand.

I reached for my coffee to try and swallow the bitter taste in my mouth. I could kiss getting a car goodbye. At least for the near future.

A warm head bumped into my leg. Scout had gotten up and was resting his head on my lap. I rubbed his ears, thinking maybe it ended up being okay that I kept him. At this rate, I wasn't going to be moving out of my Aunt Tilde's apartment for a long while. Screw Geoff.

"So what are you going to do?" Nick asked me.

I ruffled Scout's ears. "I don't know. It's his word against mine. We weren't married, just living together. There was nothing in writing as to how we would divvy up the household expenses." I took another swallow of the hot coffee. "I was such a fool."

Nick leaned against my desk, folding his arms across his chest. "You could sue him."

Startled, I looked up at him. "Sue him?"

"In small claims court."

"But … he's the attorney, not me."

Nick shrugged. "That's what small claims court is for."

"Yeah, but like I said, I have nothing in writing. It's his word against mine."

"What about household chores?" Nick asked. "How were those divided up?"

Another wave of bile rose in my throat. "I did most of the work."

"The cooking and the cleaning?"

"And the shopping. He worked a lot longer hours than me, and as he made more money, that seemed fair," my voice trailed off, and my hands clenched into fists. "That jerk. I can't believe I almost forgot. We *had* agreed that my taking care of all the household chores would make up for my paycheck being less." I didn't add I probably would have done it anyway. I liked keeping a house neat and tidy. I was overjoyed when he had proposed that arrangement.

What an absolute jerk.

Nick nodded, sipping his coffee. "Write all that down. Including how much time you spent running the household and all the things you did. Make it as comprehensive as possible."

I was already reaching for my yellow pad to scribble down what Nick suggested. "I'll do that."

"Also, don't cash the check. At least not yet."

I looked up at him. "Why?"

"He could argue you accepted the terms of his letter by cashing it. So, just to be sure, I would hang onto it for now. You can always cash it later. Unless ..." he paused delicately. "You really need that money for something."

I thought about my dashed dreams for a car. "No, there's nothing I need right away."

He nodded. "Okay. Also, I know you may want to call him and read him the riot act, but I would encourage you not to. Instead, use that time to write down everything you remember. Also, were your paychecks the only things deposited in the 'joint' account, or were there any additional funds?"

My eyes widened as I remembered my bonuses and the money I received when I sold my car. "There was other money."

He tapped the notepad. "Write all of that down, as well. Try to remember the amounts as best you can."

I made a note to myself. "Thank you, Nick. This is really helpful."

"Of course. I'm happy to help." He hesitated for a moment. "So, your severance package. Were you laid off? I didn't think the Duckworths instigated layoffs at any of their companies."

I froze, my hand squeezing my pen. The last thing I wanted to do was confess yet another area in my life where I had been an idiot, but Nick had been so helpful with Geoff, I thought it would be rude not to answer. "Officially, I resigned. But …" I lifted my head to meet his eyes. "If I hadn't, I would have been fired."

His face didn't change. "May I ask why? If I'm not prying too much."

I looked away. "I guess it's a little late for that." I blew the air out of my lungs. "I was basically the head of operations for The Duckworth Brokerage and Investments firm. My title was 'office manager,' but I was basically in charge of operations."

He took a sip of coffee. "I take it someone else had that official title."

"You guessed right. Peter Duckworth." My mouth twisted into a sour smile. "He had absolutely no qualifications or experience in operations, but the family wanted him 'involved' in the business, so there he was."

"I'm guessing he got the salary along with the title."

"I got a lot of perks," I said, not answering the question. "Nice bonuses, a couple of paid trips. I even had a company car, which is how I ended up not having one now. Geoff convinced me to sell mine and just use the company car. Anyway, one day I was going through the books when I noticed an irregularity. I thought it was a bookkeeping error, but when I started digging into it, I realized it was much bigger than that. Someone was embezzling from the company."

Nick gave me a small, knowing smile. "Let me guess—that someone was named Peter."

I picked up my coffee cup, mostly to do something with my hands. "I truly thought the family would be pleased I had discovered that Peter was stealing from them. Instead, I was the one who was essentially fired." I couldn't hide the edge in my voice.

He cocked his head. "What happened?"

I paused to take a sip of coffee. "They didn't want the PR nightmare of a Duckworth stealing from a company. They were going to handle it internally, so they didn't want to press charges. They also thought it would be … 'uncomfortable' for everyone if I kept my job, so I was given the choice—resign and get a severance check plus a recommendation or be fired. I resigned."

Except ... I didn't get the recommendation after all. It took me a while to piece it together, but once I figured it out, it was obvious.

They didn't want me staying in Riverview. I suspected if I was applying for a job in a different city, or better yet, in a different state, I would get my recommendation. But staying in Riverview was too embarrassing for them. They didn't want anyone outside of the family to know their dirty little secrets.

Nick was watching me carefully as he drank his coffee. "There might be a way to go after them. We could talk about some options, if you'd like."

It was tempting. Very tempting. Until I remembered how all the people who I thought were my friends had turned their back on me ... including the man I thought I was going to spend the rest of my life with. Did I really want to wage into battle with something that much more powerful than me?

"I don't know. I'll have to think about it. It might be best to just put it behind me and move on with my life."

Nick nodded as he sipped. "Might be. But let me know if you change your mind."

"Of course," I said, even as I doubted I would.

Chapter 14

"So, what can I do for you?" George asked, resting his ankle on his knee as he smoothed the crease in his beige pants, which he had paired with a dark-brown, short-sleeved polo shirt.

We were in George's office, which was decorated more like a den. He was a therapist, and I suspected he chose the decorum to make his clients feel more comfortable. A leather couch and chair faced each other, with a low oak coffee table between them. Bookcases filled with books and knickknacks lined the walls. The only thing that made it look remotely like an office was the heavy wooden desk pushed back into the corner and a couple of wooden cabinets directly behind the executive chair.

"It's about Hal Jarrett," Nick said. We were sitting next to each other on the couch, and George was in the chair across from us.

George's eyes widened. "Hal Jarrett. That's not what I was expecting." He shifted his gaze to me, his look more appraising. "I don't think Nick spelled out what you do, either. Are you a journalist?"

"A private detective," Nick answered smoothly, giving me a meaningful look. I kept my mouth shut, but I wasn't happy about it. Not only was I not a private detective, but I was also fairly certain the Redemption Detective Agency wasn't a legal agency, either. I made a mental note to ask Aunt Tilde again about getting a proper license.

George's eyebrows went up. "A private detective? Really? I thought he confessed."

"He did," Nick said. "But his mother hired us to look into his case to see if there was anything we could do."

George's face cleared. "She thinks he's innocent."

Nick inclined his head. "So if there's anything you can share about Hal or Rocco with us, that would be really helpful."

George hummed under his breath as he leaned forward to fill a glass of water from the pitcher in the center of the coffee table. "I don't know how helpful I can be, especially since I don't understand what happened either. But I'll share what I can."

"You knew them both, right?" Nick asked, digging his notebook and pen out of his leather briefcase.

George nodded as he took a sip. "I did. Since sophomore year. We were on the same dorm floor, and then we lived together junior year."

Nick rested his notepad on his knee. "Oh, I didn't realize you were all roommates."

"Only for one year," George said, his eyes fixed on the notepad. "There were five of us living in one of those houses that really ought to be condemned." A faint smile touched his lips at the memory.

"You didn't get along?" Nick asked.

"No, we got along fine. But it was five college guys living together. The place was always a disaster. And someone was always drinking a beer ... usually multiple someones." He shrugged. "After spending a year living in the library when I wanted to get any studying done, I decided I needed a different living arrangement. Although, to be fair, we all did. That house was pretty bad. Bob and I ended up rooming together, while Hal, Rocco, and Mikey found a different apartment."

"But you were still friends?"

George shifted in his seat. "Of course. We still hung out, went to the same parties. It was all pretty normal."

"What was Hal and Rocco's relationship like?"

George hesitated as he picked at some invisible lint on his pants. "The first two years I knew them, they got along great. They did everything together. It wasn't until the middle of our senior year that I thought something might be wrong."

"Do you know what happened?"

George shook his head. "It wasn't like there was a big blowout or anything. They just stopped hanging out together. I would see one or the other at the Union or library or party, and if I asked where the other one was, I'd get a vague answer. I finally asked Hal about it, but he just said everything was fine. I knew it wasn't, but if he didn't want to talk about it, what could you do?"

Nick tapped his pen on his notepad. "So you have no idea what really happened between them?"

George hesitated again. "Not really."

Nick's eyes sharpened. "That sounds like you know something."

George made a face. "No, I really don't. It was just …" He looked around the room and let out a sigh. "So we were at a New Year's Eve party. All of us. Hal, Rocco, Fern …"

"Rocco's girlfriend?" Nick asked.

"Yes, that's her." He paused again and rubbed his forehead. "I feel like I'm gossiping here, because I really don't know what happened, but I think Hal and Fern had a falling out."

Nick gave him a surprised look. "Hal and *Fern* had a falling out?"

George nodded. "They were always friends. Hal and Fern, I mean. Anyway, we were at that party together, and I was headed to the kitchen for another drink when I saw Fern burst in from the hallway. It was clear she had been crying, and drinking. Her makeup was smeared. I assumed she and Rocco had a fight and gave her a wide berth, but a few minutes later, I saw Hal appear from the same place Fern had. And he looked pissed."

Nick frowned. "What do you think they were fighting about?"

George held a hand up. "Are you kidding? I didn't want any part of that. At the time, I assumed it was something stupid because they both had way too much to drink. But later, after … well, after everything happened, I wondered if it was something else."

"What do you mean?" Nick asked.

George chewed on his bottom lip. "I wondered if maybe the reason why Hal and Rocco weren't getting along was because Hal and Fern were no longer getting along."

Nick sat back on the couch and rubbed his chin. "But even if that were the case, why would Hal kill Rocco?"

George shook his head. "I haven't a clue. I agree it makes no sense, but it's the only thing I can think of."

Nick mulled that over for a moment before jotting down a few notes. "Were you at the party?"

George nodded. "I was, but there's really nothing I can tell you. For most of the night, I was in the back room playing cards with four other guys. I barely saw either Hal or Rocco until … after … you know."

A shadow passed over Nick's face. "I'm truly sorry for your loss. I hope you know I'm not trying to open up old wounds …"

George waved his hand. "No, no. It's fine. I wish there was something I could do to help. I can only imagine what Hal's mother is going through." He paused for a moment, and his face turned pensive. "Although to be honest, I wouldn't mind knowing why Hal did it. I never would have dreamed Hal had that sort of violence in him. Just goes to show you, you truly never know anyone. Not really."

***

"What do you think happened between Hal and Fern at that party?" I asked Nick as soon as we left George's office.

"I have no idea," Nick said. "But even if they did have a huge fight, I don't see why Hal would kill Rocco over it."

"Unless Hal and Rocco were fighting over Fern," I said, chewing on my bottom lip. "And things got out of hand."

"You think they got into a fight because Rocco was upset that his girlfriend and best friend weren't getting along?" Nick shot me a skeptical look as he unlocked the car door.

"We don't know why Hal and Fern were fighting," I said. "Maybe whatever they were fighting about wasn't just between Hal and Fern, but Hal and Rocco, too."

Nick pondered that as he slid into the driver's seat. "That's possible."

I thought about Fern's demeanor when we spoke to her—how small and frail she seemed, sitting across from us. "We know she was lying about something. Maybe that's it."

"Could be," Nick said, backing out of the parking space.

"Although she did seem like she truly cared for Hal," I mused, remembering how upset she had gotten when she thought something might have happened to Hal in prison. "If they had a falling out, like George said, would she still consider him a friend?"

"Maybe she felt guilty," Nick said. "Especially if that fight was the reason why Hal killed Rocco."

"Or maybe the fight was about Rocco," I said. "Maybe Fern was trying to smooth things over between Hal and Rocco, and Hal wasn't having any of it."

"Possibly," Nick said, but his voice was skeptical. "But I doubt it."

"Why? The timing fits that scenario better than Hal and Fern's falling out causing Hal and Rocco to stop being friends," I argued. "It sounds like Hal and Rocco's relationship started deteriorating in the summer, but it was New Year's Eve when he and Fern had that fight. That's about six months after Hal and Rocco started not getting along."

"Well, to be fair, we don't know if that party was the first time Hal and Fern had a fight," Nick said.

"But George hadn't seen them fight before," I said.

"Exactly. George hadn't seen them fight. Which doesn't mean they hadn't. It just means George hadn't seen it," Nick said. "George also said he didn't see Hal or Rocco much after they moved into different rentals, so it's very possible the rift between Hal and Fern started long before George saw anything."

Ugh. Nick had a point. I drummed my fingers against the armrest in frustration. "What we really need to do is ask Fern," I said. "Too bad we didn't interview George first. Then we could have asked her about it when we met with her. Maybe we should just swing by her job again and ask her directly about that fight."

Nick glanced over at me, smiling faintly. "We're not the cops, Emily. I think there's a limit to how much we can bug her at her job."

"True." I frowned. "Maybe we should show up at her house, then. Do we have her address?"

"I think it's a little too soon to talk to her again," Nick said. "We don't want her to shut down completely, and she might, if we push her too much. Plus, at this point, we don't have much to go on. She could just say George was mistaken or lying or misunderstood what he saw, and there wouldn't be much we could counter with."

I sat back in my seat. "You're probably right."

"Has anyone gone through all the notes that Greta gave us? I wonder if Fern mentioned this fight with Hal to anyone else?"

"Aunt Tilde has it. I think she and Mildred were going to go through it together. Speaking of Mildred ..." I said, remembering what I had been meaning to ask him.

"Uh oh," Nick said, shooting me a sideways look.

"Does Mildred dislike you so much because you acted out in her classroom? Or is there something more than that?"

"She likes me," Nick said. I shot him a look. He grinned. "Sort of."

"If that's Mildred 'sort of' liking someone, I would hate to see how she treats someone she hates."

Nick laughed. "Alright, you got me. It probably has less to do with how I was in her classroom and more to do with ... ah ... what happened when she set me up with one of her friend's daughters."

I stared at him, aghast. "You let her set you up?"

His cheeks were stained a light pink. "I thought it was harmless. Ms. Schmidt ... Mildred was so incessant, and just like Tilde was so helpful to me when I was a teenager, Mildred helped me, too. She talked to my teachers, got me some tutoring ... I don't know if I would have gotten into college without her stepping in to help me get my grades up. Anyway, a few years ago when I moved back to Redemption, she wanted to set me up with her friend's daughter. Swore we would be a perfect match."

"And you weren't?" I guessed.

"Not even close. She was nice enough, but there was nothing there. No sparks, nothing. Although, to be fair, I'm not really a settle down sort of guy, so it was really doomed from the beginning." He raked one of his hands through his hair. "We went out a few times, and I was always a perfect gentleman. Even though I knew the relationship was going nowhere after the first date, I thought it would be better if we went out a few times. Then I could tell Ms. Sch ... Mildred, that we tried, but it wasn't a fit."

"I take it that wasn't the right decision after all," I said as we parked the car in front of the Redemption Detective Agency.

"Alas, no. Apparently, she read the multiple dates as me being more interested than I was, so when I stopped calling, she was really upset and hurt. And then Mildred was upset and hurt. So, it was a mess." He turned the car off and faced me. "Speaking of being set up, have you gone out with Jack yet?" His voice was casual, but I could see tension in his hands.

"Jerome," I corrected. "And no, there's been no date, but not for a lack of trying. At least on Mildred's side. Although now, after hearing your story, I'm even less excited about meeting him."

Nick flashed me a grin. "Well, if my troubles help you, then they would be worth it."

I rolled my eyes and opened the door, trying to ignore how every time he grinned at me, my stomach flipped upside down.

Emily, your life is complicated enough right now, I scolded myself. *The last thing you need is a new relationship. Especially with a "not a settle down sort of guy."*

Unfortunately for me, my stomach didn't seem to be listening.

Chapter 15

"Mark my words: Fern is mixed up in this sorry affair somehow," Mildred said, tapping a finger on the pile of paper and folders stacked on her desk. "In fact, it wouldn't surprise me at all if she was the one who killed Rocco."

All of us stared at Mildred, who was sitting with her back ramrod straight as she looked each one of us in the eyes, her expression disapproving. Again, I found myself sympathizing with any child caught misbehaving in her class.

We were having our first official team meeting, which meant we were all in attendance—me, Mildred, Aunt Tilde, and Nora. Nick was also present, as was Smoke, who had positioned himself as far as possible from Scout and Sherlock. Between the five of us, we had contacted nearly everyone on the list Greta had given us, as well as gone through all the paperwork and files. I had compiled our notes into one document and made copies for each of us, which had impressed the rest of the team. I refrained from saying they might not be all that impressed once they read some of the notes, like Mildred's declarations that every single person she talked to was definitely hiding something, along with a few notes as to what she thought each one might be hiding, and Nora's musings that Rocco's friend Dan sounded very cute and she intended to find out whether he was single or not.

"Why would Fern kill Rocco?" Nora asked, her voice more like a squeak. I wonder if she too felt like she was eight years old and about to get punished for something. "According to Nick and Emily, Fern wanted to marry Rocco."

"Just because Fern wanted to marry Rocco doesn't mean she also didn't want to kill him," Mildred said. "Why do you think the cops always look at the spouse first?"

"There's some truth to that," Aunt Tilde said. "I know there have been members of my family I've wanted to murder."

I shifted uncomfortably in my chair, hoping that didn't extend to nieces.

"That's exactly what I'm talking about," Mildred said.

"But why?" Nora persisted. "I know it happens, but there still needs to be a reason."

"There could be lots of reasons," Mildred said. "Maybe he was cheating on her."

"Oh, well, if that's the case, I could see that," Nora said. "That happened to me once ... one of my boyfriends cheated on me, and I definitely wanted to kill him."

"Cheating would be a strong motivation for murder," Aunt Tilde said. "Passions are high, and sometimes bad things can happen. Especially when alcohol is involved."

"Here's what I think happened," Mildred said. "Fern confronted Rocco about his cheating. Maybe she even caught him with another girl at the party. They got into a huge fight, and she hit him and accidentally killed him. Case closed."

"I could see that," Nora said, nodding.

"Wait a minute," I said, holding up a hand and hoping the meeting hadn't gone so off the rails, I couldn't get it back. "There's no evidence that Rocco was cheating on Fern. We can't just make up stories out of nothing. We're a detective agency; we're supposed to follow the evidence."

Mildred sniffed. "Men cheat. That should be enough evidence."

"Actually," Nick said. "BOTH men and women cheat. We could just as easily say that Fern was the cheater."

"Nonsense," Mildred said. "If Fern was the one who was cheating, then Rocco would have killed her, not the other way around."

"Maybe they got into a fight over Fern's cheating, and Fern got so upset with Rocco, she hit him and accidentally killed him," Nick said. "Or ... maybe they were both cheating."

"Okay, now you're being ridiculous," Mildred said. "If they were both cheating, they could just break up. One wouldn't kill the other."

"Are you sure about that?" Nick asked.

Mildred opened her mouth, then shut it with a "hmph."

"Let's put aside Fern and Rocco's relationship for a moment," I said. "IF Fern killed Rocco, why did Hal confess?"

There was a long pause. "Hal was always too nice," Mildred finally said.

"I don't think anyone is *that* nice … to go to jail for something they didn't do," I said.

Mildred looked at me with surprise. "Well, why do *you* think he confessed to a crime he didn't do?"

"I don't think he did," I said.

Mildred's eyes widened. "What? You think Hal is a murderer?" Her voice was appalled.

"No, I think it was an accident," I said. "Exactly what Hal said. He and Rocco got into a fight, the fight escalated, and Rocco ended up dead."

"But if you think he's guilty, why are you even helping us investigate?" Mildred demanded.

Why indeed? I had wondered about that myself. More than once. "Look, I agree there is something not quite right about this case. It doesn't make sense why Hal won't tell anyone what the fight was about, but whatever it was, I think it was building between them for a while. If that's the case, why not tell people? Or at the very least, why not tell his mother? So, there are things that don't make sense, and maybe if we actually discover the truth, I'm hoping some good will come out of it. Maybe it will give his mother some peace. If we're lucky, maybe we'll find something that will help Hal get out of prison sooner. Doubtful, but possible."

Even though everything I said was true, what I didn't add was how curious I had become about this case. Why would Hal hide the reason behind the fight? It made no sense to me. I wasn't exactly proud of my morbid curiosity, but it was there, just the same.

"I'd like to go back to why Mildred thinks Fern is involved," Nick said, his voice casual. He held a hand up as Mildred opened her mouth. "Other than Rocco was cheating on her." Mildred closed her mouth with a snap and shot him a dirty look.

"Fine," she said, rustling through her notes. "It was Gemini, Fern's friend."

I straightened up. "What did Gemini say?" Mildred's notes about her conversation hadn't been terribly illuminating, and I had wanted to ask Mildred for more details.

She adjusted her glasses as she peered at her notes. "Gemini was hiding something," she said, her voice solemn.

I struggled to not roll my eyes. "What did she say that made you think that?"

"And did she say anything about Fern's relationship with either Hal or Rocco?" Nick asked.

"She didn't say much about Rocco," Mildred said, skimming her notes. "Although she wasn't a fan."

"Why wasn't she a fan?" Nick asked.

"She didn't really say, other than she thought Fern could do better." She looked up and shot us all a meaningful look. "She didn't like the way Rocco treated Fern."

"I would agree with that. Rocco shouldn't have been cheating on Fern," Nora said.

Nick gave Nora an exasperated look. "Did Gemini say Rocco was cheating on her?"

"Well, no," Mildred had to admit. "But she also didn't like Hal."

"Why didn't she like Hal?" I asked.

Mildred pressed her lips together. "She didn't give a lot of specifics … basically said she thought he was manipulating her. Getting into her head."

Nick glanced at me, and I could tell he was thinking the same thing I was—what Gemini was saying was tracking with what George had said.

"But it wasn't just Rocco and Hal," Mildred continued, her brow furrowing as she studied her notes. "Fern was also acting strange."

"Strange how?" Nick asked.

"After Rocco was killed, Fern just sort of … shut down. Gemini kept trying to reach out to her—invite her out for dinner or to study together or even just to be with her—but Fern kept declining all her invitations. And it wasn't just Gemini. Fern quit hanging out with all her friends. The only person she spent time with was her brother. Otherwise, she kept to herself."

"Well, the man she thought she was going to marry was killed," I said. "Grief can do strange things to people."

"True," Mildred said. "Which is why Gemini tried to reach out a year after it happened, too, but Fern still didn't seem interested in being friends. Gemini even asked if she had done something wrong, but Fern said no, she just didn't have much time for friends. Claimed to be too busy with her career."

"That's a little weird," Nick said.

"I agree," I said, thinking of Fern working in the town of Redemption. I wondered what could be so important with her job that she wouldn't have time for friends.

The phone rang, actually all four phones, which reminded me again to sort that issue out. I answered it before the other three started arguing about who should answer it. "The Redemption Detective Agency, Emily speaking."

"Em! Finally."

"Deena!" I had been playing phone tag with my best friend since I moved to Redemption, leaving multiple messages. "I'm so glad to hear your voice."

"Who is Deena?" Mildred asked.

"Is that a new client?" Nora asked.

I waved for them to be quiet before turning to angle my body away. I wished I could take the phone somewhere else for more privacy, but at least Nick and Aunt Tilde seemed to figure out this was a personal call, and I could hear them distracting Mildred and Nora.

"Is this a bad time?"

"No, no, it's fine. I'm just happy you called."

"Yeah, I'm sorry." Deena's voice was regretful. "It's been crazy here for the past couple of weeks. I just haven't had a moment, which is why I thought I'd try you at work, as I finally have a few free minutes."

"I'm glad you did," I said.

"So, how's the new job? Actually, what is the new job?" Deena asked.

"Um … it's good," I said, shifting further toward the wall.

Deena chuckled. "I take it your aunt is there."

"You guessed right," I said.

"Well, you know Riverview isn't that far away if you need a break," she said. "I miss you."

"I miss you too," I said.

There was a funny little pause, during which I expected Deena to invite me to stay with her again, but instead she said, "Well, even though it's a bummer you aren't here anymore, it was probably lucky that you have someone you could stay with in Redemption. A fresh start, and all of that."

This was so different from what Deena was saying before I left that for a moment, I was completely speechless. Instantly, I was back in my apartment in Riverview, well Geoff's apartment, calling the people who I thought were my friends only to be given a cold shoulder. "Deena, what's going on?"

"Nothing. What do you mean?" Her voice sounded forced.

"Did Eric say something to you?" Eric, her boyfriend who also worked with Geoff, lived with her, more or less.

"What? Why would you ask that?" This seemed like a careful avoidance of the question.

All the pieces started clicking together in my mind. All the messages I had left, not just on her voicemail, but also with Eric, and how when she finally called me back, she was at work. Over the years of us being friends, I could count on one hand the number of times she called me while at work. "Eric doesn't like you talking to me, does he?"

"It's not like that," she said, which sounded to me like it was exactly like that. "Everything is just a little … weird right now. In a few months, it will all settle down."

A coldness had sunk into the pit of my stomach. I squeezed my eyes shut and took a deep breath. "It's because of Geoff, isn't it?"

"No!" She practically shouted the word, causing me to jerk back. But she must have realized how she sounded because she quickly softened her voice. "No, it has nothing to do with that lying scumbag."

The coldness turned to ice in my gut. As much as it would suck to lose my best friend because her boyfriend forced her to choose my ex, it somehow wasn't as bad as what I was afraid she was going to say. "Then why?"

There was a long pause. "Look, you must know," her voice had turned pleading. "The Duckworths are one of their largest clients. They can't afford to upset them."

My hand gripped the phone receiver tightly. Would I ever be able to return to Riverview? I was starting to think I was going to be forever exiled just for being a good employee doing her job. "If that's the case, I doubt a few months are going to make a difference."

"It will." The confidence in her voice sounded forced. "We just need a little time. That's all. In a few months, no one is going to remember what happened."

As much as I wanted to believe Deena, I had a sick feeling in my stomach that the Duckworths were never going to forget. But maybe she was right, though, and Eric would be less likely to care. "I appreciate you calling me and letting me know. I don't want to become a problem in your relationship."

"No, that's not why I called. Em, you're never a bother. We're always going to be friends, you hear me?" Her voice was fierce, and I wondered if she was trying to convince herself. "But maybe for the next few months, if you need to call me, call me at work."

"I thought your boss frowned at you taking personal calls."

"It will be fine," she said. "Just as long as I make up the time later, it's not a problem."

Great. Basically, if I called my best friend over the next few months, I would be responsible for making her work overtime. I was so frustrated, I wanted to scream, but if I did, I would have to answer a bunch of questions I had no desire to answer.

Man, my life sucked.

How could I have gotten myself into such a mess? I never in a million years dreamed that working for the Duckworths would put everything in my life at risk. Not just my career, but my friends and family, too.

Family. Another thought slammed into me so hard that for a moment, I felt like I couldn't breathe. "That's the real reason why

Geoff broke up with me, isn't it? Because of his job?" All that talk about us not being a good match was a lie. He just didn't want his relationship with me to hurt his chance at a promotion. He was willing to toss me aside to keep his career safe.

I was going to be sick.

"Geoff is a jerk." Her voice was vicious. "But there's something else I have to tell you."

Something in her voice made my back stiffen—like I was going to like what she was about to say even less than what she already had said. "What?" My voice was wary.

She sucked in a breath. "A couple of nights ago, we were having dinner with another couple. Coworkers of Eric's. Geoff was at the same restaurant." She paused. "He was with his secretary."

My mind flashed to his secretary—tall, thin, blonde, with big breasts. Geoff had sworn he never noticed her looks because she was so efficient at her job. I forced myself to swallow. "Well, it's not that big of a surprise. It's not like we're dating anymore."

"No, Emily, you don't understand." Her tone was full of regret. "The other couple … they didn't know I knew you. They made a remark about how at least Geoff no longer had to hide his relationship, since he officially had broken up with his 'old girlfriend.'"

Girlfriend. Not even fiancé, even though that was supposedly what I was. Could this day get even worse? "Did Eric know?"

"Eric quickly changed the subject as soon as he saw my face, but …" there was another long pause. "I'm so sorry, Em. I gave him hell about it, if that makes any difference. Told him he should have been honest, but … well … he's a guy. What can I say?"

Even though I appreciated Deena defending me, it wasn't Eric's fault. He was never my friend. I wouldn't actually expect him to tell me the truth. "Well, I guess now at least I know what Geoff was doing during all of those late nights." I kept my voice light, trying to hide my pain.

"Oh Emily …"

"I have to go," I said abruptly, sure if I stayed on the call any longer, I would cry. Or scream. Or maybe both. "And you should get back to work as well."

"Call me," she insisted. "I mean it."

"I will," I said, lying through my teeth. I wasn't going to call her. She didn't need the baggage of having to lie to her boyfriend.

And I didn't need the reminder of everything I had lost.

I hung the phone up and pressed my fingers to the corners of my eyes, willing myself not to cry.

"Everything okay?" Nick asked.

I plastered a smile on my face and turned around. "Of course. Just my friend Deena. She's been so busy, she hadn't been able to call me sooner. She's just had a lot going on." I was babbling, and I forced myself to slow down. I could feel Nick's eyes boring into me, and I made a point of not looking at him.

"She can call anytime," Aunt Tilde said. "You know I don't care if you take personal calls at work. I trust you."

I bit my lip and looked down at the packet of notes. "So, where were we?" I forced a lightness into my voice.

"Trying to figure out what to do next," Mildred grumbled. "We know people are lying, but we don't know how to make them tell the truth."

"Other than going back to Fern to ask about her argument with Hal, we're out of ideas," Nick said. "And I think we need something more before going back to Fern."

"You should let me talk to her. I can get her to talk," Mildred said.

That was almost enough to make me smile. I started flipping through my notes, trying to distract myself and get my head back into the case. I saw the words "spring break trip" and paused.

"Hey, does anyone know what happened during Hal and Rocco's last spring break trip?" I asked.

The other four shook their heads. "No, other than it seemed to make things worse rather than better," Aunt Tilde said.

I tapped the piece of paper. "Was it just those two? Or did anyone else go with them?"

Understanding dawned on Aunt Tilde's face as she picked up the phone. "I'm almost sure they were with someone. I'll call Greta to see if she knows who."

Chapter 16

"The Redemption Detective Agency, eh?" Josh said as he looked around our front office, a little taken aback by the number of people and animals squashed inside. "Do you have a card? I sometimes have clients in need of a detective agency."

Aunt Tilde's eyes lit up as she started pawing through her desk. "Oh, of course. Let me find one for you."

Josh, who had accompanied Hal and Rocco on their infamous spring break trip, lived in Riverview, but that week, he had happened to be in Redemption for a couple of client meetings and offered to stop by our office. Which was a good thing, as we were having trouble deciding who should question him. Everyone agreed I should be there, as it was my idea, as well as Nick, although I wasn't clear why he got a pass. Nora wanted to be there, as she had never questioned someone in person and thought it sounded like fun. Mildred told her it wasn't meant to be fun; it was supposed to be serious. But regardless, Mildred absolutely needed to be there as she had a sixth sense when people were lying. Aunt Tilde told her that was nonsense, and it might have devolved into a nasty argument if Josh hadn't offered to swing by.

Scout moseyed up to Josh and sniffed him, wagging his tail. Josh gave him a reluctant pat. He wore a suit, a nice one, dark blue with a light-blue tie. I imagined he didn't want to get dog hair on his clothes. His reddish-brown hair was cut neatly, and he was clean-shaven.

Aunt Tilde handed him a card and offered him a chair. Nick was leaning against the desk in the corner of the room, and I was sitting in a folding chair I had found in the back of the kitchen, now that it felt safe to venture back there.

"So, how can I help you?" Josh asked, trying to make eye contact with all of us.

"It's about Hal Jarrett," Aunt Tilde said.

Josh's eyebrows went up. "Hal Jarrett. That's a name I haven't heard in a while." He shifted in his seat, crossing one ankle over his knee. "I'm not sure how I can help you though. My understand is that he confessed to killing Rocco."

"He did, but we've been hired to look into his case to see if there are any irregularities," Nick said.

Josh looked confused. "Any irregularities? What does that mean? He did it, right?"

"That's what we're looking into," Nick said.

"It's possible someone else was involved," Mildred said.

A look of horror flashed over Nick's face, but he quickly smothered it. Luckily, Josh was too busy staring at Mildred in shock to notice. "Someone else? You mean Hal may not have killed Rocco?"

"There are a lot of things we're looking into that we're not in a position to talk about right now," Nick said quickly, shooting Mildred a hard look. She glared at him, then closed her mouth. "We're hoping you can answer a few questions for us."

"Sure, however I can help," Josh said. "Nothing would make me happier than to learn that Hal didn't kill Rocco. I liked them both … they were my friends." His expression was haunted, and he quickly dropped his gaze.

"You were with them for spring break, right? The last one before the party?" Nick asked.

Josh nodded, reaching for the glass of water that Aunt Tilde had given him. "South Padre Island. It was a tradition. We went every year."

Nick nodded. "It seems that Hal and Rocco weren't getting along that senior year, and whatever happened during that spring break trip exasperated it."

"It definitely did," Josh said, nodding.

"Do you know what happened?"

Josh shrugged. "I would imagine it was because Rocco cheated on Fern with a one-night stand."

Silence. Then Mildred slammed her hand down on her desk. "I knew it! Didn't I tell you Rocco was cheating on Fern?"

Josh was staring at all of us. "What, you didn't know?"

"No, it wasn't in any of the police reports," Aunt Tilde said, shuffling through the papers on her desk. "At least the ones we were given."

"I thought it was basically an open secret," Josh said, leaning back in his chair. "Just like Hal having a huge crush on Fern."

Another long silence. Josh looked around at us again. "I guess that wasn't in the police reports either."

"No, and no one else said anything," Aunt Tilde fretted.

"Well, to be fair, Hal hid it pretty well," Josh said. "I only know because he told me one night after he had a few too many drinks."

"Do you know when it started?"

Josh frowned as he played with his water glass. "I think Hal was in love with Fern the moment he met her, but Rocco was his best friend. He never wanted to do anything that would hurt him. Or Fern. If they were truly in love, Hal wasn't going to get in the middle of it."

Nick's eyes sharpened. "If?"

Josh hesitated, as if searching for the right words. "Look, this is just my opinion, okay? I never had a conversation with Rocco about Fern. But …" he paused again. "I think Rocco was starting to lose interest in her."

"And why do you think that?"

"Just the way he was acting. He wasn't bringing Fern to as many parties or out for drinks, even if some of the other guys brought their girlfriends. I didn't see them study together anymore, not like they used to. I actually thought they had broken up."

"They should have broken up," Mildred said disapprovingly. "If he wasn't interested in her anymore, he should have done the right thing."

Josh inclined his head. "True, but Rocco did like to have his cake and eat it too. He liked having a girlfriend when it was convenient for him, and Fern didn't appear to object."

I shifted uncomfortably in my seat, suddenly recognizing a little bit of myself in that statement.

"Do you know when Rocco started cheating on Fern?" Nick asked.

"I have no idea," Josh said. "For all I know, spring break was the only time, but I kind of doubt it."

"So spring break, Rocco had a fling ..."

"Yeah," Josh said. "Hal was not happy. He told Rocco he shouldn't be doing stuff like that to Fern. Rocco told him to mind his own business, and that was that. The two basically ignored each other for the rest of the trip."

"Did you talk to either of them after?"

Josh let out a laugh. "Are you kidding? I couldn't wait for that trip to be over. I stayed as far away from the drama as possible. I figured they would eventually work it out, but I didn't need to be involved."

"Were you at the party the night Rocco was killed?" Nick asked, even though we were pretty sure he hadn't been, which was why he wasn't on any interview list.

Josh shook his head. "No. I had to go home that weekend for a family thing, but to be honest, I probably would have found another excuse not to go once I found out that both Hal and Rocco were going to be there."

"And Fern," Mildred said.

"And Fern," Josh agreed. "Way too much drama for me. Although ..." his face shifted back to the haunted expression from earlier. "I never in a million years dreamed it would have played out the way it did."

"So, when you heard that Hal killed Rocco, what did you think?" Nick asked.

"Initially? That it was a mistake," Josh said. "Hal isn't the type to beat someone up or get into a bar fight. Rocco wasn't either, for that matter. I could totally see those two yelling at each other, especially if they were both drunk, and maybe one taking a swing at the other, but that would be it. Although I suppose if Hal actually caught Rocco with a girl ..." he paused. "Maybe if it was something like that, Hal punched Rocco, and then it all went horribly wrong."

"What if it was someone else?" Mildred asked. "Someone like ... Fern?"

Nick glared at her.

"Or someone else," Aunt Tilde jumped in. "Would there be

anyone else who would be upset enough by Rocco's cheating to do something about it?"

"Well, yes, definitely Fern," Josh said. "Her friend ... what's her name?"

"Gemini?" Aunt Tilde asked.

"Yeah, her. I could definitely see her jumping into a fight, especially to protect Fern," Josh said, rubbing his chin. "Maybe Fern's brother, as well, although I don't know him very well. There may have been others. Fern has this ... innocent quality about her. Makes you want to protect her. I could definitely see one of the other guys punching Rocco to defend Fern's honor."

I pictured Fern sitting hunched over in the conference room chair, so small and fragile. I could see it, as well, Fern bringing out that protective instinct in a man.

Although it didn't explain why Hal would have confessed to someone else's crime.

"Do you know anyone else who might have wanted to kill Rocco?" Nick asked. "Someone who wasn't connected to Fern?"

"Other than the girl who Rocco was cheating on Fern with?" Josh gave a slanted smile. "Fern was at the party, right? If Rocco was cheating on Fern, and didn't tell the girl about Fern, and the girl found out at the party, I could see that being a problem."

I hadn't considered that ... that it might not have had anything to do with Fern, but rather with the girl Rocco was seeing. If he was really seeing another girl, that is.

"Oh, the tangled webs we weave," Mildred said, shaking her head sadly.

"Anyone else?" Aunt Tilde asked.

"No one is coming to mind. At least not right now," Josh said. "Rocco was one of those guys you always called when you wanted to go out and get drunk. He was a party guy. A lot of fun. Other than his extracurricular activities with women, he wasn't really someone who had enemies. He was the guy who had a million friends. Not very close friends, mind you, but lots of them."

I knew exactly the kind of guy Josh was describing. The life of the party—fun, but shallow. Not the type you would expect to be killed by one of his friends, even if it was an accident.

Was it possible someone else killed him, and Hal was taking the fall for some reason?

Chapter 17

The four of us were back at the Riverview prison, crammed into the small conference room as we waited for Hal to join us.

At least, we all hoped he would. His parting words to us at our last visit were to leave him alone and not go digging into his case. Which we didn't do.

I hoped that wasn't a mistake.

After a very long discussion once Josh left, we finally agreed that speaking to Hal before Fern made the most sense. Even though Mildred objected strenuously. She was convinced Fern was guilty and all we needed was some sort of *Matlock* moment, where we accused her, and she would break down in tears and confess.

Nick thought that was a risky move. If she didn't break down, then all we would have done was show our hand, and it would be that much harder to get a confession from her in the future. "Keep in mind, if she is guilty, she's letting Hal rot in prison for a crime she committed. That's not the behavior of a woman who is going to be easily trapped."

Mildred reluctantly agreed, but only after we agreed that all four of us would interview Hal. Nick only wanted it to be him and me, as he thought Hal might be more likely to open up to a couple of us rather than a whole team, but Mildred informed him if he left her behind, she was going to march right over to Fern's office.

In the end, we all piled into the pink Cadillac for a road trip to Riverview.

I had mixed feelings about all four of us in one car versus Nick and I driving alone. On one hand, I liked chatting with Nick. He entertained me with a lot of funny stories about some of his legal cases, but he also asked me questions and listened to me.

On the other hand, it was better to not spend time alone with Nick. I had no intention of dating him, or anyone, for that matter, but I especially didn't want to date another lawyer. I'd had my fill of attorneys after Geoff, thank you very much.

"What's taking him so long?" Mildred muttered, smoothing out her blue and white polka-dot short-sleeve blouse. Her hair was freshly set, as she had an early-morning beauty appointment. Her floral perfume was strong enough to cover up the stink of the prison.

Aunt Tilde worriedly fiddled with her hair. "Greta told me he's been in a foul mood lately. We should have told the guard we have good news for him."

Nick gave her a look. "He was pretty clear he didn't want us looking into what happened. I doubt he would consider it 'good news' that we ignored his wishes."

"But we might be able to get him out of here," Aunt Tilde said. "That should put him in a better mood."

Before Nick could answer, the guard was opening the door with a clang. Hal's expression immediately soured. "I told you guys not to come back. Guard …"

"Wait," Nick said, jumping to his feet. "We have news. Good news, about your mom's lawyer."

I blinked. While Nick had done some impressive lawyer-speak, I'd never seen him out and out lie.

Hal stared at him before nodding to the guard. "Never mind. I'll stay for now." He shuffled over and sat down in the chair in front of us as the guard shut the door. "What news? Is she getting her money back?"

"Yes, but the amount is still in negotiation," Nick said. "I don't think it will be the full amount, but I should be able to get most of it returned to her."

I blinked again. Was this true? And if it was, when had Nick had time to talk to this other attorney? Both Mildred and Aunt Tilde looked as flabbergasted as I was, and I really hoped for Nick's sake, he wasn't just bluffing to get Hal to stay.

Hal closed his eyes and slumped back in his chair. "Oh, thank you," he said. "That takes such a load off of me, to know she won't be completely destitute because of me."

"Trust me, the pleasure was all mine," Nick said. "If there's one thing I hate more than anything, it's unscrupulous lawyers."

Hal nodded and straightened up. "I owe you, big time. Does my mother know? She didn't say anything to me."

"She doesn't know yet," Nick said. "But there is something you can do for me."

"Sure, anything," Hal said. "Well, anything that I can do from in here." He lifted a hand to gesture around the room.

Nick smiled. "I just need a few answers. That's all."

It was like a mask slammed down over Hal's face. His eyes were suspicious as he studied Nick. "What kind of questions?"

Nick's smile remained fixed on his face. "Just what happened the night Rocco died." He leaned forward slightly, his eyes sharpening. "What really happened."

Hal started working his jaw. "I told you to leave it alone," he hissed. "I confessed. I'm guilty. Just leave it alone." He started to get up again, but Nick held a hand out.

"Look, do you want your mom to let this go? Really let it go and not hire another charlatan who tells her what she wants to hear? Then you need to help me. You need to tell me the truth of what happened that night. Otherwise, I guarantee she's going to spend every penny she has trying to prove your innocence."

Hal glared at Nick. A muscle jumped in his forehead, and I could practically feel how much he wanted to lash out at Nick.

"You know I'm telling you the truth," Nick said, his voice soft. "Do you want this to end or not?"

Hal stayed where he was for another moment, grinding his teeth before collapsing back into his chair. "Fine. What do you want to know?"

"Why you're still protecting ... ouch," Mildred yelped, giving Aunt Tilde a hard look. Aunt Tilde's expression was pure innocence, like butter wouldn't melt in her mouth.

"Protecting who?" Even though his voice sounded angry, his face was full of fear. "What are you talking about?"

"If you just tell us what you and Rocco were arguing about ..." Nick started to say, but Hal's eyes were fixed on Mildred.

"Who do you think I'm protecting?" he demanded.

Mildred's face softened and she reached forward to pat his arm.

"I know you have a good heart, but you don't need to protect Rocco anymore. You can tell us the truth."

"No!" He jerked his arm away like she had burned him. "That's what you don't understand. I'm not good. I am guilty."

Mildred's eyes went wide. "What are you talking about? You didn't kill anyone! That's not possible. I don't believe it."

He lowered his head and started shaking it. I could have sworn I saw the sheen of tears in his eyes. "I did though, Ms. Schmidt. I killed Rocco."

***

There was a long moment of silence. "I don't believe it," Mildred finally said, her voice no-nonsense. "You must be mistaken. That's simply not possible."

"Mildred," Aunt Tilde said softly, putting a hand on her arm. "Let the boy tell us what happened."

Hal didn't lift his head. "How much do you know?"

"You were in love with Fern, Rocco's girlfriend," Nick said. Hal flinched but kept his head down. "And he was cheating on her."

He let out a long sigh. "I told her he wasn't good for her. I told her. But she wouldn't listen. She thought …" He took another deep breath and lifted his head. "If I thought she would be happy, truly happy, with Rocco, I swear to you I would have walked away. I wouldn't have done anything to upset her happiness. But …"

"She wasn't happy," Mildred said softly.

He turned to look at her, his eyes full of grief. "It wasn't always like that. In the beginning, I think Rocco did truly care for her. But that last year? She was a habit. A crutch. That summer, I could tell he was losing interest. I tried to convince him to do the right thing. To break up with her. But he wouldn't listen. He liked having her around as a backup." His voice was bitter.

"That's why you stopped hanging out," Nick said.

Hal nodded miserably. "I just couldn't. If he was going to treat a woman like that, a woman he had claimed to be in love with at one point, I couldn't be friends with him. But I also couldn't ignore Fern. I tried to talk to her multiple times, but she wouldn't listen.

She was convinced they were just going through a rough patch, and if she just hung on, it would all be okay."

"But it wasn't," Mildred said.

He exhaled. "No, it wasn't."

"So why did you go to spring break with him?" Nick asked.

He made a face. "I shouldn't have. I should have backed out. I almost did. But I figured it would be the last spring break I would ever have in my life, and what could it hurt? We would all hang out and drink too much like always." His voice drifted off, and he stared at the wall.

"But that's not what happened," Nick prompted.

"No." Hal scrubbed at his eyes. "It was stupid, I know. It wasn't like it was a huge surprise Rocco wasn't faithful. A part of me figured he wasn't. But seeing it somehow …" His eyes had a faraway look. "Something shifted in me. I was so angry. At him, at Fern, at myself. I was full of rage. And that didn't change even after we returned home."

"So what did you do with all that rage?" Nick asked.

Hal let out a bark of laughter that had no humor in it. "Buried it. As best as I could. It didn't work, though. It just festered inside me, getting stronger and stronger. Until the night of the party."

There was another long pause before Nick quietly said, "Tell us about that night."

Hal made a disgusted face. "I don't know what I was thinking. I knew Rocco would be there, and probably Fern as well. But I was just so … angry. I think I wanted to get into a fight with Rocco, if for nothing else then to just release the pressure building inside me.

"I started drinking before the party, so I was already buzzed and not thinking straight when I arrived. I immediately continued drinking, so when I saw Fern, I already had way more than I should have, especially in the mood I was in."

He took a deep breath and let it out before raising his head to meet all our eyes, a resigned look on his face. "I told her. The truth. That Rocco was cheating on her."

This was so not what I thought he was going to say. I was prepared to hear his confession of killing Rocco in cold blood. This seemed anticlimactic.

"What did she say?" Nick asked, although I had the feeling his thoughts had gone in the same direction as mine.

"She didn't want to believe me," Hal said. "She told me I was a liar. She screamed at me that I was just jealous and trying to break them up. She punched me in the chest as she said it, but I didn't defend myself. Because she was right, I was jealous, and I did want to break them up. But I was also telling the truth. And I think, deep down, she knew I was telling the truth.

"She ran out of the room, and I didn't follow her. I went into the back room where a few guys were playing cards. I watched them as I finished my drink, and then I went to refill it. And that's when I saw it."

"Saw what?" Nick asked when it seemed like Hal wasn't going to continue.

"Fern," he said, his eyes glistening. "She ran past the kitchen, and I could tell she was upset. Really upset. She disappeared into the crowd. I started to follow her until I saw that she was with one of her friends. I still couldn't let it go, though. I had to know what happened."

He paused and roughly scrubbed at his face. "I found Rocco in one of the bedrooms." His voice was so quiet, it was difficult to hear him. "He was still alive, but barely. His head … the blood …" his voice trailed off again as he rubbed his eyes. "His mouth was moving, like he was trying to talk, but nothing was coming out. I …" he swallowed hard. "I knelt down and asked him what happened, but he couldn't answer. He just stared at me, his eyes begging for me to call for help. To do something to save him."

He looked around at us, his eyes dull and resigned. "But I didn't. I did nothing except watch him die."

There was a long moment of silence as we digested his words.

Aunt Tilde was the first to speak. "Is that why you think you're guilty?" she asked, her voice soft. "Because you didn't call for help?"

"You don't understand," he bit out, his anger rushing out of him as if telling the truth had uncorked something inside him. "In that moment, I wanted him to die! I was glad because I thought … I thought …" he buried his face in his hands.

Mildred reached out again to put a gnarled hand on his arm.

"You shouldn't beat yourself up. You're human, and you were protecting the woman you love."

"How can I live with myself?" Hal asked, his voice muffled by his face in his hands. "Never in a million years did I ever think I would not try and save someone!"

"You were drunk," Aunt Tilde said. "You weren't thinking straight. But more than that, I don't think there was anything you could do. I don't think there was anything anyone could have done. It was too late. So even if you would have tried to call for help, it wouldn't have made any difference, other than he might have ended up dying alone."

"So, in a way, it was good you stayed with him," Mildred said. "He didn't die alone."

Hal kept his hands over his eyes, and I had a feeling he didn't find that particularly comforting.

"If that's what happened, you shouldn't be in jail," Nick said. "Whoever pushed Rocco is the one responsible for his death, not you."

Hal finally lifted his head, his expression bleak. "It doesn't matter. I can only be responsible for my actions, not anyone else's. And my actions are reprehensible."

"Maybe," Nick said. "But there's an argument to be made that you're taking too much responsibility for something that isn't your fault. And because you're doing that, you're preventing the person who truly is guilty from taking responsibility for their actions."

Hal bit his lips, his expression pensive.

"We need to get you out of here," Mildred said. "We need to tell the district attorney …"

Hal started shaking his head violently. "No! We can't do that."

Mildred wrinkled her forehead. "But why? People need to know the truth."

"No, they can't know the truth." His voice was panicked. "Just like you can't tell my mother."

"Why can't we tell your mother?" Aunt Tilde asked. "You didn't kill that boy …"

"Because the truth is so much worse," he practically shouted. "What would she think of me if she knew I did nothing while

Rocco died? She can't know that. It's bad enough she thinks it was an accident, but to find out I did nothing but watch him die?"

"Hal, your mother loves you," Aunt Tilde said. "She will love you no matter what. You owe her the truth."

"And you owe it to yourself to tell the truth," I said, speaking for the first time. Hal's head swung over to me, his eyes full of pain. I held his gaze, feeling like I could have been saying the exact same words to myself. "I know how it feels to hide a secret from the people who love you. It's not fair to them, and it's not fair to you either. All it's doing is eating you up inside, and for what? Your mother knows you're human and make mistakes. You need to have faith in her that she can handle this. Quite honestly, the fact you haven't told her the truth hurts her more than the actual truth."

There was another moment of silence after I finished speaking. Everyone was still staring at me, although Hal's expression had shifted to more thoughtful. Aunt Tilde was looking at me with what appeared to be approval. Nick just flashed me a grin and winked at me.

I kept my eyes on Hal and tried to keep myself from blushing.

"You might have a point," Hal finally said. "I need to think about it, but even if you're right, then what? What do I do?"

"I've got some ideas," Nick said.

Chapter 18

I rubbed my sweaty hands against my cream, linen shorts, trying to ignore the three pairs of eyes burning a hole into the back of my light-pink shirt as I reached for the door to the Redemption town hall.

We had spent most of the drive back from Riverview arguing about who should talk to Fern. Mildred thought it should be her and spent most of the ride insisting it. "You two had your shot, and you didn't get anything out of her," Mildred sniffed. "It's my turn to try."

"She's going to be even more wary of someone new," Nick said. "It needs to be us. I know it's not much, but we've established a little rapport with her. If she's going to confess to anyone, it will be us."

I cleared my throat. "Actually, it should just be me."

Everyone turned to look at me—even Aunt Tilde, who should have been watching the road. "You?" Mildred asked.

"Alone?" Nick asked.

In my mind's eye, I saw again Fern sitting huddled in the chair, looking so frail and pathetic. I saw the little coy glances she kept shooting at Nick from beneath her lashes. I thought about Hal sitting in a jail cell even though in his heart he knew Fern was the guilty one. I thought about how she dropped her friendship with Gemini.

While I couldn't be sure, and I didn't understand why she would have stayed with Rocco when he seemed to have completely lost interest in her, she seemed like the type of woman who was used to wrapping men around her little finger. Which meant I didn't think she would tell Nick the truth.

Not that I was sure I would get the truth out of her either, but I thought being alone was our best shot.

"I feel like I can talk to her, woman to woman," I said. "Especially since we both share a similar history of bad judgement in our relationships."

I could feel Nick's eyes on me, and I made a point to not look at him. This was embarrassing enough, but if there was a way I could leverage my own cluelessness to right a wrong, it would be worth it.

Mildred's eyebrows shot up as she peered at me from over the front seat. "Emily, that's all in the past. It's all going to get better for you."

"I agree," Nick said.

Mildred glared at him. "Don't think I don't have my eye on you."

Nick held his hands up in mock surrender.

"Then it's settled," Aunt Tilde said. "Emily is going to handle Fern. Alone." She eyed Mildred, who did not look happy.

"But I can help," Mildred said. "Emily shouldn't be there by herself. She needs backup."

"No, she doesn't," Aunt Tilde said firmly. "She will be fine."

Eventually, Mildred acquiesced. Barely. Aunt Tilde was pulling into the parking lot before Mildred seemed to finally accept that she was outnumbered.

My hands were still sweaty as I grasped the door handle, but I ordered myself to relax. I was absolutely going to fail if I didn't get myself under control.

I asked the same receptionist as last time if I could speak to Fern, then waited awkwardly in the lobby for her to appear. When she finally did, she stopped dead, a wary look on her face. I gave her a smile that I hoped didn't look as forced as it felt.

She approached me cautiously, her expression apprehensive. "What do you want?"

I cleared my throat. "Can we talk? Privately."

She didn't move. "I'm working."

"It's important."

She stood her ground, her eyes narrowing. "My job is important, too."

Well, this wasn't going well. For a moment, I contemplated

backing off and waiting to approach her again after work, but then I pictured Mildred's smug expression as she said, "I told you so," if I failed.

So I took a step toward her and lowered my voice. "As important as going to jail for murder?"

She blanched, all the blood draining from her face. "What do you …" she broke off, looked around hurriedly, then gestured for me to follow her to that same conference room. I found myself wondering how much it was actually used for city business.

"What do you want?" she demanded as soon as she shut the door behind me. "Money? I'll tell you right now, I don't have any."

I stared at her in confusion. "Wait. Do you think I'm here to … blackmail you?"

She crossed her arms across her chest and lifted her chin. Her white, lacy shirt was a little too big for her, along with her navy slacks that needed a belt to stay on her slim waist. "Well, aren't you?"

I stared at her in disbelief. "No. I'm here to right a wrong. A wrong that you shouldn't have let happen."

She cringed and looked away. "It wasn't supposed to happen. None of this was supposed to happen." She uncrossed her arms and waved her hands. "I should be married and starting a family. Not here working a dead-end government job."

"So what happened?"

She eyed me, looking me up and down. "Are you wearing a wire?"

I blinked, taken aback. "No, I'm not wearing a wire."

"Are you working with the police?"

"No, nothing like that."

Her eyes narrowed. "What about your boyfriend? The *lawyer*." She dragged the word out. "Where is he?"

I cocked my head and studied her. Despite her aggressiveness, I sensed something beneath the anger and belligerence.

Fear.

"My fiancé cheated on me," I blurted out. Her eyes widened. "More than that, he tricked me." I was surprised by how bitter I sounded. "Kicked me out of my apartment, lied to me, stole my life's savings. I get it. I get how angry you must have been. But …" I took a step closer, looking directly into her eyes. "That doesn't mean you should let Hal take the blame for what you did."

She looked startled. "Me? What are you …" her mouth snapped shut, and she turned her face away, but not before I saw the truth in her eyes.

"You weren't alone," I said.

She turned away from me. "You need to go."

"I'm not going to go until you tell me what happened that night," I said. "Who was with you? Who was the one who killed Rocco?" My mind flipped through the people on the list. I was missing something, and I knew it.

"Hal killed Rocco," she said, but her voice wavered. "He pled guilty."

"To a crime he didn't commit, and you know it," I retorted, still frantically searching for clues. What was I missing? It was right on the tip of my tongue.

"Why would he do that?" she asked. "If he wasn't guilty, why would he plead guilty and go to the jail then?"

"Oh, for Pete's sake, you can't be that naïve," I said. "Hal loves you. That's why."

Her face seemed to collapse on itself. She took a step back, hugging her arms across her body.

"How could you do that to him? Knowing that?"

"I …" she opened her mouth and closed it. "I didn't want to. You have to believe me. I didn't want any of this to happen."

"Did you even care about Hal?" I asked. "Or did you just use him because you knew how he felt about you?"

Her head snapped up. "Of course I care about him," she hissed. "Maybe, if I had met him first instead of Rocco, things would have been different. But I was with Rocco. I had spent nearly four years with him. I couldn't give that up! We were supposed to be getting married. He promised me we would!"

"But he wasn't going to keep that promise," I said. "You know that, don't you?"

She bit her lip as she turned away. "I thought … I thought if I could just talk to him. I knew … I'm not an idiot. I knew he was losing interest. But I still loved him. At least I thought I did. And I thought I could get him back, if he would just give me a chance. That was all I wanted … a chance." She turned to look at me, her eyes pleading with me to understand.

"But he didn't want to give you a chance," I said.

"It wasn't like that," she said. "He was furious with Hal. Said he shouldn't have told me. It didn't mean anything. He was drunk and it just … happened. I told him I would forgive him, but things needed to change. I needed things to be different. He …" she chewed on her lip.

"What?"

"He just said, 'Sure, babe. Whatever you need.'" Her voice was full of disgust. "He was so … dismissive. I knew then that it was over. He wasn't going to change. He was going to keep stringing me along as he continued to treat me like crap."

"So you hit him," I said.

"No, I told you, I didn't touch him," she insisted, and I almost believed her, except her eyes kept darting around the room.

And then it hit me.

"It was your brother, wasn't it?"

Her face went completely white. Her hands flew up, and for a moment, I thought she was going to faint. "What?" she squeaked. "No … no, Felix didn't have anything to do …"

"So was Felix there when you confronted Rocco? Or did it happen after?" I asked.

She closed her eyes as her knees buckled beneath her as she slowly collapsed to the floor. "He didn't mean to kill him."

I knelt down, too, so I was facing her. "Tell me the truth, Fern. I know this secret has been eating you up inside. Has it been eating Felix up as well?"

She stared at me, her eyes listless, her knees bent at a strange angle beneath her, like she was a broken doll. "He's drinking. A lot. So much that he can't work anymore, other than some off-the-books construction jobs. I'm worried about him." She plucked nervously at her pants.

"Maybe you both need to tell the truth," I said.

Her entire body trembled, and for a moment, I didn't think she would, but then she let out a shuddering sigh and started to speak. "After Hal told me what happened on spring break, I cornered Rocco and told him what I knew. I already told you how that conversation went. I was so upset after, I was practically in tears. Felix was the one who found me in that state. I wasn't going to tell him, but ..." she looked at me, her eye glistening. "He's my brother. My twin. He could tell something was wrong, which is why he came looking for me."

"So he went looking for Rocco," I said.

"He was furious," Fern said. "I tried to tell him not to make a big deal out of it, at least not at the party, but it was too late. He found Rocco as he was leaving the bathroom and dragged him into one of the bedrooms to talk to him. It didn't ..." She bit her lip again. "It didn't go well."

"They fought?"

"Not exactly. Rocco told Felix this was none of his business. That it was between me and him. Felix said as he was my brother, so it did concern him. Rocco told him to back off before things got bad."

She went silent, but I could picture the rest.

"He didn't back off, did he?"

Her eyes were wet, and her makeup was smeared. "He didn't mean to kill him." Her voice was a whisper. "I didn't even know what happened until Hal burst into the living room, yelling that Rocco was dead. I thought ... I don't know what I thought. That Rocco was drunk and fell and hit his head. That's what everyone was saying initially, but then I looked over and met Felix's eyes, and ..." she swallowed hard. "I knew the truth."

She looked so defeated, it was tough not to feel sorry for her. But then I pictured Hal in his orange jumpsuit serving a sentence for a crime he didn't commit, and my sympathy turned sour. "Why didn't you say something to the cops?"

Her voice was monotone. "He was my brother. My twin. How could I possibly betray him like that? I told myself maybe I was wrong. Maybe it was Hal after all. An accident gone wrong. But ..." she shook her head, and her voice dropped even lower. "In retrospect, you're right. I should have told the truth."

Chapter 19

"I've got good news," Aunt Tilde sang out as she burst into the Redemption Detective Agency. "Hal is officially exonerated! He's being released from prison!"

I swiveled in my desk chair to face her and clapped my hands. "That's wonderful news. Nick, did you hear?" Nick, who had dropped by over his lunch hour to work on the kitchen, poked his head out of the swinging door so Aunt Tilde could share the news with him.

"I'm so glad," Nick said. "What about Felix?"

Her expression became more solemn. "He confessed. To everything. It sounds like it was almost a relief for him to finally tell the truth."

"What about Fern?" I asked. At first, Fern hadn't wanted to get the cops involved. "Let me talk to him," she kept saying. "He needs to be the one to turn himself in." While that might be true for Felix's mental state, I wasn't convinced that either Fern would talk to him, or that Felix would make the right choice. In the end, I gave her forty-eight hours to talk to her brother, or I would go to the cops. She agreed, and the next day, Felix turned himself in.

"She's upset, of course. It's her brother, after all," Aunt Tilde said.

"I meant, is she getting charged with anything?" I asked.

She shook her head. "Felix insists she didn't know anything. He acted alone."

While I wasn't surprised that Felix was taking all the blame, a part of me felt like it was a little unfair. Yet again, Fern was going to allow another man to save her from her actions.

On the other hand, picturing Fern's broken body sprawled out on the conference floor in my mind's eye, maybe she had suffered enough.

"But there's more good news," Aunt Tilde said, digging an envelope out of her oversized purse and handing it to me. "I have your paycheck!"

"Paycheck?" I gave her a funny look. "But there's no money coming in."

"But there is," Aunt Tilde said, pointing at the envelope. "That's from Greta. Thanks to Nick getting some of her money back from that terrible lawyer, she decided to pass it along to us as a thank you for getting Hal out of the jail."

Well, that was a positive sign. Money from an actual client. Maybe this business wasn't going to be such a disaster after all. I pulled out the accounting ledger. "I'll deposit it today. And have you discussed salaries with Nora and Mildred?" I braced myself, hoping I wasn't going to be tasked with having that conversation with them. For that matter, I had no idea what my salary was supposed to be either, although quite honestly, I didn't think it should be much. I was already getting quite a bit of perks.

Aunt Tilde waved her hand. "Don't worry about them. That money is yours."

I blinked at her. "I don't understand."

"That's your paycheck. Or, at least, the start of it." She came closer, her expression becoming serious. "Look, I know we didn't talk about a salary for you, and to be honest, I don't know what is even fair for what you bring to this role. So, I figured we could play it a little by ear, at least at the beginning, and you'll get what the clients pay us."

"But …" I was so flabbergasted, I didn't even know what to say. "That's not how this works. There are other expenses you need to pay with this money …"

"That's all covered, don't worry about that," Aunt Tilde said.

"But Mildred and Nora need something," I said. "They put time in …"

"Mildred is bored," Aunt Tilde said. "And she has a pension. She doesn't need the money. And Nora has her own business, so don't worry about her."

"But I still don't think it's fair," I said, remembering how Nick also wasn't getting paid for any of this.

Aunt Tilde patted my hand. "You have nothing to worry about. I already spoke to both of them and they agree. Until we get this business off the ground, you should get the majority of the money. Once we've got a regular income stream, then we can revisit our arrangement."

I still didn't think it was fair, but it also didn't seem like I was going to win this argument.

"Oh, and I have more good news," Aunt Tilde said, pulling out another envelope from her purse and handing it to me. This one was from the State of Wisconsin. I eyed her as I opened it.

It was a private detective license.

"See, The Redemption Detective Agency is now official," Aunt Tilde said proudly.

I examined the license, feeling like a huge weight had just rolled off my shoulders. "Why didn't you tell me you were getting one?" I asked.

She shrugged and looked a little embarrassed. "I had to pass a test, and I wasn't sure if I was going to or not. So, I thought it would be better to surprise you."

I glanced at the license, then back at Aunt Tilde. "What would have happened if you hadn't passed?"

She flapped her hands. "Who cares? I passed with flying colors. Oh, and I have one more surprise for you." She went to the front door, opened it, and dragged something inside. "Tada!"

It was a sign that read "The Redemption Detective Agency" in big black letters with a red magnifying glass on the end.

"You like it?" she asked, but there was something about her expression, so eager and hopeful, that made me think she wasn't really asking about the sign.

She was asking about all of it. My apartment, my job, my life.

"I do," I said, and I meant it.

Her face relaxed, and she beamed at me. "I've got some people coming later today to put it up. Oh, and I almost forgot. This came for you." She extracted yet another envelope out of her purse, which made me wonder just how many envelopes she had stuffed in there, and handed it to me.

It was from Geoff's law firm.

My stomach plummeted as I tore it open. This couldn't be good. Why else would he be sending me something so soon?

"Is everything okay?" Aunt Tilde asked as I yanked the contents out of the envelope.

"Not sure," I said. A check fluttered out, and I leaned over to scoop it up. I looked at the amount, then blinked. And blinked again.

Geoff had sent a check for twelve thousand dollars.

Was this a mistake? It had to be. I unfolded the letter and began reading.

Emily,

As requested, please find the balance of your final paycheck and severance package. I expect this should conclude our business.

On a personal note, I find it very hurtful you would hire an attorney to personally attack me. How could you have done that to me, your former fiancé? Have you no shame? Clearly, I was right to end our relationship, as you are obviously not stable. Please do not contact me again.

Cordially,
Geoff

I had to read it three times over to take it in. Attorney? What was he talking about …

A loud crash from the kitchen made me jump. No, he couldn't have.

Could he?

"Emily?" Aunt Tilde asked again.

"Just give me a second," I said, getting up from my desk and heading toward the kitchen. Nick was inside, rubbing the back of his neck as he studied a piece of plywood on the floor. He had rolled up the sleeves of his button-down shirt, showing an expanse of well-muscled arms. When he saw me, he flashed me an embarrassed grin. "Sorry. Making too much noise?"

I leaned against the doorjamb. "Actually, I just wanted to tell you I got a letter from Geoff."

Nick's eyebrows went up. "Oh?"

"Yes. Apparently, he doesn't like my attorney very much."

Nick chuckled. "I'm sure there are a lot of attorneys he doesn't like, especially ones more competent than he is."

I folded my arms across my chest. "That may be the case, but the funny thing is, I don't remember hiring an attorney."

He shrugged. "Maybe he just needed an excuse to do the right thing. Did he send anything else with that letter?"

"A check."

"For everything he owes you?"

"Yes."

He nodded before reaching down to pick up the plywood. "Good. That's settled then."

I watched him as he measured the piece of wood, frowning slightly as he made another mark on it. "Thank you."

He glanced up at me and flashed me one of his charming grins that made my heart flutter in my chest. "You're welcome."

I wasn't sure what else to say. I wanted to ask him why he would do that for me, but the words were stuck in my throat. Instead, I inclined my head and started to leave.

"Oh, Emily?" His voice was suspiciously casual.

I paused. "What?"

He kept his eyes on the plywood. "The offer is still open, if there's anyone else in Riverview who might need a little nudge to do the right thing."

I froze, my hand still on the door, my mind immediately going to the Duckworths. I thought about the fear in Deena's voice and how quickly my life fell apart after I was dismissed from my job.

I swallowed hard. "I'll keep that in mind."

He nodded. "No rush. Just … whenever you're ready."

"I appreciate it," I said, even as I wondered if I would ever be ready. I still hadn't told my sister the truth, after all. Did I really want to take on that fight?

***

A few days later on a late Friday afternoon, I was sitting at my desk, trying to tune out Mildred and Aunt Tilde bickering in the corner of the room. Or maybe they were gossiping. It was sometimes hard to tell with those two.

We had gotten a few new client inquiries, courtesy of Greta and how grateful she was for our help. I also was figuring out an advertising budget, something a little more effective than hanging flyers in various locations, and trying not to think about Nick.

At first, I had half-expected him to ask me out. I mean, he helped me get my money back—that must mean something. Right?

But then I reminded myself as to what he said to Hal about how much he hated unscrupulous lawyers. That was probably all this was; he hated injustice and wanted to straighten that out whenever he could. Plus, it was clear he wanted to pick a fight with the Duckworths, even if I wasn't so keen.

So, no. I shouldn't assume he was interested in me, even though he had single-handedly made it so I could go car shopping this weekend. Aunt Tilde told me I might as well buy a new car, as it would cost too much to fix her old one.

But still. There was something about the way he looked at me that made me wonder, even as I tried to tell myself there was nothing between us.

The bell at the door tinkled, and Nick strode in, almost as if I had conjured him by thinking about him. I could feel my cheeks flush as he grinned at me. "Just needed to check on a couple of things before the weekend."

"Of course," I stammered before burying myself in my spreadsheet again. When I looked up, it was to see Mildred staring at me.

Abruptly, she stood up. "A word, Emily?"

Aunt Tilde looked between us, a slightly alarmed expression. "Mildred," she started to say, but Mildred waved her off. "In private?"

Slowly, I rose to my feet, not liking where this was going. It seemed Mildred had reluctantly set her issues with Nick aside after he had helped Greta get her money back from her lawyer issue, but maybe not.

I followed her down the hallway to where the bathrooms were. As I trailed behind her, my eyes started to water from the strength of her floral perfume. If I wasn't close to her, I could sometimes forget how much she used.

When she reached the end of the hallway, she turned toward me, crossing her arms and tapping her foot. "Emily, what are you doing?"

I took a step back, a little taken aback by how upset she was. "What are you talking about?"

She flung her hands up. "You know what I mean! You're flirting with Nick!"

I flushed a deeper shade of red. "I wasn't flirting with Nick ..."

"Don't lie to me," she interrupted, her voice full of disgust. "Or yourself. You're too smart for that."

I shut my mouth, unsure of what to say to that.

She paused, closing her eyes and sucking in a deep breath. "Look," she said, her voice quieter. "I get it. He's very good looking, not to mention a real charmer. But," her voice rose and she took a step closer to me, her eyes intense, "he WILL break your heart. Emily, I know you don't know me very well, but trust me. I've known Nick his entire life. I'm not saying he's a bad guy. He's not. He does have a good heart. But that doesn't mean he won't break yours. He's not the type of guy who wants to settle down."

Her voice rang in my ears as I remembered Nick's very own words: "not a settling down type of guy."

Maybe Mildred was right. Maybe this idea that Nick was going to ask me out was just me being silly and romantic.

Mildred must have seen something in my face because her look softened. "Look, it's not your fault. Nick has ... a way with women. You shouldn't blame yourself. You just need to be careful. I know you already had one heartbreak ... you don't need another."

"No," I mumbled. "I don't."

She reached out to pat my arm. "You're going to be just fine. You're a good girl, Emily. And I should know; I'm an excellent judge of character." Before I could respond, she brushed by me and headed back to the main office.

Apparently, the "talk" was over. I followed her out, trying to avoid meeting everyone's eyes as I slunk back to my desk.

"Everything fine?" Aunt Tilde called out.

"Peachy," I muttered and tried to focus on my budget spreadsheet.

A male voice cleared his throat in front of me. I looked up to see Nick standing in front of my desk, an unsure expression on his face. "Emily, I was wondering if I could talk to you."

"Emily," Mildred said.

I ignored her. "What do you need?"

He shifted from one foot to another. "Well, I was wondering …"

The front doorbell chimed, and a woman burst in. "Nick! There you are."

Nick's jaw dropped. "Trisha? What are you doing here?"

Trisha was drop-dead gorgeous. She had long, black curly hair that reached halfway down her back, dark-blue eyes, and porcelain skin. She had huge breasts, a tiny waist, and ample hips.

In short, she was perfect.

She let out a tinkling laugh. "Silly. Your secretary told me you'd be here."

Secretary? The image of Nick's empty office flashed through my mind until I remembered how Nick had said his assistant was out that week.

"Oh," Nick said faintly as Trisha gave him a kiss on the cheek, wiped the lipstick off, then tucked her arm through his.

"A detective agency," she mused, looking around before spotting Sherlock and Scout. "With mascots."

"That's right," Aunt Tilde said. Mildred shot me a meaningful look that I tried not to notice.

"Maybe you can help find my aunt's dog," she said brightly. "Since you obviously like dogs." Scout, for his part, didn't seem like he cared for her. He stayed where he was on his dog bed. "He's been missing for a year now," she continued, not realizing she had been doggy snubbed.

"We're not animal control," I snapped, my voice harsher than I intended. Trisha looked at me in surprise.

"We'd be happy to look into it," Aunt Tilde rushed in, shooting me a look. "Although finding a lost dog after a year of being missing might be challenging."

Her expression was puzzled. "You just cleared a man who confessed, right? That's like impossible, isn't it? Finding a lost dog should be easy for you."

Aunt Tilde looked flummoxed. "Um …"

The front door jingled its merry tune again, interrupting Aunt Tilde. "Sorry, is this the Redemption Detective Agency?"

I turned and did a double take. A very attractive man was standing uncomfortably in the door. He had chestnut brown hair, deep brown eyes with thick lashes, and an innocent puppy dog look.

"Jerome," Mildred said, leaping to her feet. "I'm so glad you're here. Emily, meet Jerome."

This was *Jerome*? The chemistry teacher who needed Mildred's help finding a date? My brain felt like it was breaking.

He turned and gave me a smile that lit up his entire face. From the corner of my eye, I saw Nick frown. "Emily! Mildred had told me so much about you. I know this is short notice, but I was wondering if you had plans for the night."

"Oh! A blind date," Trisha shrieked, digging her elbow into Nick's chest. "Maybe if you two end up a couple, we can all go out on a double date? Wouldn't that be fun, Nick?"

Nick muttered something that didn't sound like an agreement.

I looked back at Jerome, taking in his neatly combed and parted hair, his clean-shaven face, and how neat and tidy his pressed white polo and khakis were. Nick, on the other hand, was a little rumpled. His pale blue button-down shirt was wrinkled, and he had a five o'clock shadow.

Even better, Jerome wasn't another lawyer.

I turned to him, squaring my shoulders and flashing a smile at him. From the corner of my eye, I saw Aunt Tilde sag, but I ignored her as well. "As it turns out, I have no plans for tonight."

He blinked, seeming a little taken aback at my response. "Oh. Well, would you like to have dinner?"

Trisha was bouncing up and down next to Nick, who was looking sullen and angry, while Aunt Tilde looked resigned, and

Mildred looked smug. I refused to acknowledge any of them and instead smiled even more brightly at Jerome. "I would love to."

A Word From Michele

We're just getting the party started with *The Redemption Detective Agency*. Keep going with Book 2, *The Mysterious Case of the Missing Dog Walker*.

Preorder your copy right here:
mpwnovels.com/r/q/bmotivedogwalkwide

The Redemption Detective Agency is a spin-off from the *The Charlie Kingsley Mysteries*. If you want to see where it all began, take a look at *Loch Ness Murder*.

***

You can also check out exclusive bonus content for *The Redemption Detective Agency* here.

The bonus content reveals hints, clues, and sneak peeks you won't get just by reading the books, so you'll definitely want to check it out. You're going to discover a side of Redemption that is only available here.

MPWnovels.com/r/q/redemption-agency-bonus

***

If you enjoyed *The Mysterious Case of the Missing Motive*, it would be wonderful if you would take a few minutes to leave a review and rating on Goodreads:
goodreads.com/book/show/218654558-the-mysterious-case-of-the-missing-motive
or Bookbub:
bookbub.com/books/the-mysterious-case-of-the-missing-motive-the-redemption-detective-agency-book-1-by-michele-pariza-wacek
(Feel free to follow me on any of those platforms as well.) I thank you and other readers will thank you (as your reviews will help other readers find my books.)

All my series are interconnected and related, and if you'd like to learn more about them, take a look at my website MPWNovels. com. You'll also discover lots of other fun things such as short stories, deleted scenes, giveaways, recipes, puzzles and more.

I've also included a sneak peek of *Loch Ness Murder* if you'd like to check it out. Just turn the page to get started.

Loch Ness Murder - Chapter 1

"Wait, which monster did you say you wanted to document again?"

Nancy's voice floated across the lobby as I pulled open the door to the Redemption Inn, a charming bed and breakfast. It was built like a log cabin, with hardwood floors, polished oak furniture, and cozy quilts. Nancy, the owner, was one of my tea clients. She stood eying the two men standing in front of the check-in desk, her silver glasses perched on her nose.

"The ones at Angel's Lake," said the first man eagerly, dropping his bag so he could paw through a notebook he carried under his arm. He wore an ill-fitting brown suit that matched his badly cut hair and smudged glasses.

"Oh, you mean Locky," Nancy said, reaching up to adjust her hair, which was as brittle as old straw thanks to many bad perm and color jobs.

The second man blinked confusedly at her. He too was in a rumpled suit, but his was blue, and his tie was askew, as though he had been pulling on it. "'Locky'?"

"Yeah. You know how the Loch Ness Monster is called 'Nessie'? We call ours 'Locky.'"

Both men just stared at her. "That doesn't make any sense," Brown Suit said, his voice agitated. "The Loch Ness Monster is called that because it lives in a loch in Scotland that's fed by the River Ness."

Now it was Nancy's turn to return the confused blinking. "Loch? You mean a lake."

"No, I mean a loch, although it is an old Gaelic word for 'lake,'" Brown Suit said. "It's a common misconception."

"I didn't know that," Nancy said. "You really do learn something new every day."

"But that's why the name doesn't make sense," Brown Suit continued, his agitation rising. "You might as well call him 'Lakey.'"

"Um," Nancy uttered.

"And furthermore," Brown Suit continued, "this lake is called 'Angel's Lake,' not 'Loch Ness.' It doesn't make sense to name a monster after a lake it doesn't even live in." At that, he flapped his arms wildly, scattering his papers everywhere.

Nancy stared at him, clearly torn as to whether she should help him pick up his papers or just change the subject. "Um, well, you make a good point. Unfortunately, I didn't have anything to do with the naming convention of our local Loch Ness ... errr ... lake monster."

"It's important to accurately identify creatures, so you can refer to them by their proper name," Blue Suit said. "If you aren't calling them by their correct name, how will you know how to handle them?"

"People don't realize how many sea creatures there are," Brown Suit interjected as he awkwardly gathered his papers. "I realize this is a freshwater lake and not an ocean, but it's certainly possible something from the sea learned to adapt to fresh water."

"Precisely," Blue Suit agreed. "It may not even be a lake monster. What if it's a water nymph or sprite ... or a selkie? Calling it 'Locky' would make even less sense."

"Actually, the correct term is 'naiads,' not 'water nymphs,'" Brown Suit corrected, giving Blue Suit the side-eye.

Blue Suit flushed. "I was using the term 'water nymphs' because it is more common than 'naiads,' and I wanted to make sure everyone understood." He gestured with his head toward Nancy.

"I am familiar with naiads," Nancy said drily.

"Yes, but if we're going to insist on correct naming conventions …" Brown Suit said, ignoring Nancy.

Nancy glanced away, an eye roll imminent, but that's when she saw me.

"Charlie," she said, her voice loud as she interrupted, clearly relieved by the distraction. "I'm so glad you stopped by. I'll be with you in a minute, after I check in these two gentlemen."

The aforementioned gentlemen turned to gawk at me. Both wore thick glasses, and their eyes were wide and round as they stared.

"Oh, you're a girl," Brown Suit said matter-of-factly.

"Yes, I am," I confirmed.

"With a name like 'Charlie,' I was expecting a man," he sniffed. He turned back to Nancy. "This is why naming things properly is important. Otherwise, people can make the wrong assumptions."

"Charlie can be a girl's name, too," I said.

"There are more men named 'Charlie' than women," Brown Suit said. He kept his head down, not meeting my eyes as he fussed with his papers. "It's very confusing."

The mention of my name had clearly thrown him for a loop, and rather than being upset about it, I found myself feeling sorry for him. Actually, I was feeling sorry for everyone in the situation, including Nancy, who seemed flummoxed by this particular check-in process.

"So, you're going to investigate our lake," I said.

Brown Suit glanced up, his brow furrowed, his expression a mix of confusion and distrust, but despite all of that, his eagerness to talk about his work won out.

"It's well-documented that very few bodies are recovered from Angel's Lake," he said. "Bodies don't surface in cold, deep lakes the way they do when the water is warmer and shallower. But, my research has shown that sometimes, other factors are at play."

"Other factors," I said, nodding. "Like the naiads and water nymphs and Loch Ness Monsters?"

"Naiads and water nymphs are the same thing," Brown Suit said, his tone reproachful.

"I stand corrected," I said.

"And the Loch Ness Monster isn't an actual breed," Blue Suit continued. "It's most likely a plesiosaur."

"So, you think we might have a naiad or plesiosaur in our lake?"

"We don't know what you have. That's why we're researching it," Brown Suit said.

"It's possible there's nothing going on other than the lake being cold and deep," Blue Suit added. "But we've heard the stories and think it's worth checking out."

"What stories?" I asked. Behind the men, Nancy could no longer control it—she rolled her eyes.

Redemption, Wisconsin, is a charming little town that also has a haunted past. Back in 1888, all the adults disappeared. Only the children were left, and they all swore they had no idea what happened to the adults.

Since then, Redemption had been a hotbed of strange and mysterious events. People frequently disappeared without a trace, along with other unexplained happenings. Then there's the many haunted buildings, including my own house. There were so many stories, in fact, that even though I'd been living in the town for a few years already, I'd only heard a fraction of them, and I still couldn't keep track of them all. I really needed to start keeping a record.

"Well, the stories of Angel's Lake being haunted," Brown Suit said, flipping through his notes. "There have been sightings of a variety of creatures. Lake monsters similar to the Loch Ness, beings that look like humans in the water, which could be the naiads or selkies or sprites, or maybe even some sort of freshwater mermaid." Brown Suit's eyes gleamed from behind his glasses. "I know everyone thinks all those creatures are myths or legends, but I've discovered proof to the contrary."

"Proof?" I asked. "What sort of proof?"

Brown Suit's eyes went wide with horror. "Oh! I can't tell you that." He hugged his notes to his chest and took a step backward, as if I was about to leap forward and pry them from his arms. "It's very confidential."

"That's why we're here," Blue Suit said. "We're going to be publishing our findings soon, and we're hoping Angel's Lake will give us the final data points we need before we release it all to the world."

"What we've discovered is going to be earth-shattering," Brown Suit said. "It's going to set the scientific establishment on its head. So, we need to make sure we dot all our I's and cross our T's."

Blue Suit nodded solemnly. "We need to be prepared. It's going to be like opening Pandora's box. Once it happens, it's going to blow a lot of people's minds. So, we need irrefutable proof."

"Which we have," Brown Suit was quick to add. "But it can't hurt to have more."

"Wow, 'irrefutable proof,'" I repeated. I couldn't imagine what that could be. Photographs? Those could be doctored. Same as recordings. But whatever it was, they seemed extremely confident it would hold up to the scrutiny of the scientific community. "I'll be interested in seeing it."

"You won't be disappointed," Brown Suit assured me.

"Well, if that's the case, I hope you find what you're looking for in our little lake," I said.

From behind them, I saw Nancy roll her eyes again.

Want to keep reading? Grab your copy of *Loc Ness Murder* here: MPWNovels.com/r/bmotivelocwide

Books and series by Michele Pariza Wacek

Redemption Detective Agency
(Cozy Mysteries)
A spin-off from the Charlie Kingsley series.
https://MPWNovels.com/r/da_motive

Charlie Kingsley Mysteries
(Cozy Mysteries)
See all of Charlie's adventures here.
https://MPWnovels.com/r/ck_motive

Secrets of Redemption series
(Pychological Thrillers)
The flagship series that started it all.
https://MPWnovels.com/r/rd_motive

Mysteries of Redemption
(Psychological Thrillers)
A spin-off from the Secrets of Redemption series.
https://MPWnovels.com/r/mr_motive

Riverview Mysteries
(standalone Pychological Thrillers)
These stories take place in Riverview, which is near Redemption.
https://MPWnovels.com/r/rm_motive

Access your free exclusive bonus scenes from *The Mysterious Case of the Missing Motive* right here:
MPWnovels.com/r/q/redemption-agency-bonus/

Acknowledgements

It's a team effort to birth a book, and I'd like to take a moment to thank everyone who helped, especially my wonderful editor, Megan Yakovich, who is always so patient with me, Rea Carr for her expert proofing support, and my husband Paul, for his love and support during this sometimes-painful birthing process.

Any mistakes are mine and mine alone.

About Michele

A USA Today Bestselling, award-winning author, Michele taught herself to read at 3 years old because she wanted to write stories so badly. It took some time (and some detours) but she does spend much of her time writing stories now. Mystery stories, to be exact. They're clean and twisty, and range from psychological thrillers to cozies, with a dash of romance and supernatural thrown into the mix. If that wasn't enough, she posts lots of fun things on her blog, including short stories, puzzles, recipes and more, at MPWNovels.com.

Michele grew up in Wisconsin, (hence why all her books take place there), and still visits regularly, but she herself escaped the cold and now lives in the mountains of Prescott, Arizona with her husband and southern squirrel hunter Cassie.

When she's not writing, she's usually reading, hanging out with her dog, or watching the Food Network and imagining she's an awesome cook. (Spoiler alert, she's not. Luckily for the whole family, Mr. PW is in charge of the cooking.)

Made in the USA
Monee, IL
20 October 2024

67708204R10098